# PRAISE FOR DAVID H. HENDRICKSON

"David H. Hendrickson is one of my favorite writers."
— *USA Today* Bestselling Author
Kristine Kathryn Rusch

"One of the most diverse writers I have had the pleasure to meet."
— *USA Today* Bestselling Author
Dean Wesley Smith

"Hendrickson's first two Rabbit Labelle novels brilliantly let us experience the historical struggle of the 1960s civil rights movement through the eyes of a short, scrawny teen who loves sports, his family and friends, and doing what's right even when it's hard. In this final book in the trilogy, Rabbit's pushed to the limit with his father, his friends, and his baseball coach, even as the nation reels from a horrible tragedy that affects the people of Lynn, too. Hendrickson's created a wonderfully-imperfect hero we can't help but root for. Rabbit's struggles with anger and self-doubt, love and the pure joy of sport, are a wonderful rocket to ride. An engrossing, cathartic read."
— Terry Hayman
author of *Chasing the Minotaur*

"As teens struggle to navigate social challenges in today's society, this riveting story of teens engaged in the same struggle in the past will help today's youth see they are not alone, and there is hope for a better world now and in the future."
— Rebecca Shelley
author of *Dragonbound: Blue Dragon* and *Nikeron the Great*

"Another thoroughly enjoyable sports-based outing with heart and something to chew on after the game."
— Dory Crowe
author of *Dark Secrets*

**Also by David H. Hendrickson**

*Cracking the Ice*
*Bubba Goes for Broke*

**Rabbit Labelle Trilogy**

*Offside*
*Offensive Foul*
*Bottom of the Ninth*

**Collections**

*Shimmers and Laughs: Eight Wildly Hilarious Tales*
*Death in the Serengeti and Other Stories: Ten Tales of Crime*

**Nonfiction**

*How to Get Your Book Into Schools and Double Your Income With Volume Sales*
*Travis Roy: Quadriplegia and a Life of Purpose*

**Writing as D. H. Hendrickson**

*Body Check*
*No Defense*

# BOTTOM OF THE NINTH

## DAVID H. HENDRICKSON

Pentucket Publishing
www.pentucketpublishing.com

## Author's Note

Although this book can be read and enjoyed on its own, its events follow those of *Offside* and then *Offensive Foul*. To maximize your enjoyment, the author suggests that you read both of those books first.

Also, even though Lynn is a real city with its streets and landmarks accurately depicted, this is a work of fiction. Other than clearly identified public figures and historical incidents, all characters and events portrayed in this book are fictional and any resemblance to real people or incidents is purely coincidental. For dramatic effect, Lynn English High School is described as including ninth grade, which is true today, but was not yet the case in 1968.

*To my father, who passed away almost twenty-eight years ago,*
*But will remain in my heart for all of my days.*

# BOTTOM OF THE NINTH

## DAVID H. HENDRICKSON

# CHAPTER 1



*Monday, March 11, 1968*

I just know it's going to be a great baseball season.

It's a raw, bleak afternoon for the first day of tryouts. A biting wind whips into our faces. It's barely forty degrees and feels a lot colder, as if it's below freezing in the middle of December with spring and summer nowhere in sight.

But I'm still happily bouncing on the balls of my feet, ready to dive for an errant throw even though we're just playing catch. I'm warm enough in my gray sweatshirt and sweatpants, navy-blue Boston Red Sox cap, and cleats. I'm filled with anticipation that baseball will wipe out the sour aftertaste of what happened with the basketball team. Soon, the gray skies will turn blue, the sun will beat down hot on our necks, and the sound of the crack of the bat will fill the air. I pound my glove with my fist, hold it to my nose, and smell the sweet scent of well-oiled leather.

Twenty of us freshmen are paired off, warming up on one of the lousy middle fields here behind Lynn English High School. We're halfway between the two first-class fields close to the school and the Little League fields at the far end of the block almost a half mile from the school. The good fields, where games are held, are reserved for the varsity and JV players. They have a twenty-foot-high metal fence that extends from the backstops to divide the third-base foul area of one field from the first-base foul area of the other. Green light towers rise even higher to provide lighting for night games.

Our practice field could not be any more different. Our infield is all dirt, no grass, and its dimensions are those of a Little League field. So when I go to my shortstop position, I'll be standing in the outfield grass. Or to be more accurate, the outfield crabgrass. It's as bad as the other two fields are great. Standing five feet to my left, Charlie Watkins says what I'm thinking.

"Feels like I'm back in Little League," he says, gesturing with his free hand and shaking his head.

Charlie is my best friend from both the football and basketball teams even though I'm white and he's black. Like all of us from the basketball team, where short hair was the rule, his close-cropped hair barely pokes out from beneath his baseball cap. It's only a hint of the huge Afro he wore during football. My own hair is barely longer than a crew cut.

He catches the ball from Jessie Stackhouse, another black friend from the football team, a broad-shouldered, muscular line-backer almost six feet tall who hit like a freight train. Jessie is not only that ultimate rarity, a black hockey player, but was the varsity team's superstar even as a freshman, leading the entire league in goals scored.

"You and me and Jessie," I say, nodding in Jessie's direction, "we ain't gonna be on this field for long."

"You got that right," Charlie says with a big grin.

I'm little. Little, but quick. That's why my nickname is Rabbit. Rabbit Labelle. The varsity football coach, Coach McDonough, referred to me as *five-nothin', hundred-nothin'*, meaning not an inch over five feet tall and not an ounce over a hundred pounds, and that was accurate back then. I've grown a bit in the last few months—I'm five-one and a hundred and seven pounds—but *five-nothin', hundred-nothin'* still pretty much sums me up. I had to use my speed and quickness on the football field to avoid getting crushed by guys twice my size. I did a pretty good job of it, especially on kickoffs and punt returns, but I had a much tougher time in basketball, even before all the problems.

In baseball, though, size doesn't really matter much, so it's my best sport. I may not be able to blast home runs over the fences, but I can rip doubles and triples down the line and into the alleys, and if I only get a single, I can usually turn that into what amounts to a double with a stolen base. In the field, I can range far to my right and left, diving for ground balls and then bouncing to my feet in time to throw a bullet to first base and catch the runner.

So I have the highest of expectations for this season. I won't be like Jessie was in hockey, a superstar on the varsity, but I might be like Charlie was in basketball, eventually moving all the way up to the varsity starting lineup even as just a freshman. He had to go through a lot to get there—just because he's black—but he got there. The original basketball coach, Coach Abrams, was eventually fired for his bigotry that in the end turned violent, but he kept Charlie under his thumb, relegating him to the freshmen team no matter how many points he scored.

With any luck, the only drama for any of us will be whether we can rip a line drive down the left field line to score a runner from second. The only tension we'll feel will be bases loaded, two outs, down by a run in the bottom of the last inning.

No controversy. No hatred. No fighting. Just fun on the ball field.

It'll be great.

Coach Gilhooly, the freshman coach, blows his whistle and gathers us around, down on one knee. "We're going to start batting practice in just a minute," he says, trim in his gray LEHS warm-up suit, Lynn English stitched in maroon letters above where a pocket would be. A whistle dangles from his neck. He takes off his gray-with-maroon-letters LEHS cap, runs his fingers through his brown hair, then puts the cap back on. "But first, Coach Kowalski, the varsity coach, has a few words to say."

Coach Kowalski, who has made his way from the varsity field to ours, stands a shade under six feet tall. He's in his fifties with graying hair, bushy gray eyebrows, and a pronounced paunch hanging over his belt line. My guess is that he weighs around 230 or 240. He wears the same warm-up suit as Coach Gilhooly, but it's far less flattering, emphasizing his beer belly more than hiding it. A thick chaw of tobacco bulges inside this right cheek.

Coach Gilhooly steps back, and Coach Kowalski moves forward. A grim look covers his face.

"Before you *freshmen* take so much as your first batting practice," he says, uttering the word *freshmen* with obvious disdain, almost as if it's a disease, "I want to make one thing clear."

He pauses, and slowly scans the whole lot of us, presumably to make sure we're paying attention. He seems to stop at Charlie, off to my left, then moves on until his eyes lock on to mine. His jaw hardens. He spits brown tobacco juice onto the ground.

A shiver runs up and down my spine that has nothing to do with the gusting wind. A bitter taste forms in my mouth. Why is Coach Kowalski glaring at me? What have I done?

"This team," he finally says, "is not going to have a repeat of the shenanigans that ripped the basketball team apart."

My heart sinks, then red-hot anger flares behind my eyeballs. *Shenanigans?* Is that what he thinks of six black players and myself standing up to a blatantly bigoted coach, one who racially demeaned them and attempted to rob them of their dignity? One who said they played like…played like…well, I don't like to repeat his use of the word that begins with the letter N, and I don't mean Negro. He used it to insult them and the kind of basketball they played compared to his "superior" brand of lily-white basketball.

His use of that hateful word prompted Charlie, another black friend, Jamaal Bryant, and four other black players along with me to leave the team. I had to do it. Stand with my friends. Stand for what was right. It was a matter of dignity for my black friends. A matter of conscience for me. In the following days, we organized a protest in front of the school, one that soon included members of the NAACP, parents, and almost fifty students. It gained the attention of newspapers, including the *Boston Globe*, and even local TV stations.

A peaceful protest.

Peaceful until Abrams got his brother to organize thugs who attacked us, thugs with baseball bats who broke the bones of adults and students alike. My mother, my girlfriend, Anna, and I were lucky to escape unscathed, but others like Jamaal were not so fortunate. His broken ribs sidelined him for almost the entire remainder of the basketball season. His father suffered a broken arm, Charlie's mother a broken wrist.

*Standing up against that amounts to shenanigans?*

Standing up against Abrams was a righteous cause, as righteous on its very tiny scale as that of Dr. Martin Luther King on his grand scale as he marches down South to oppose racial segregation and injustice.

*Shenanigans?*

My blood boils. Every muscle in my body tenses. My impression of Coach Kowalski has suddenly plummeted off a cliff. He probably isn't even smart enough to tie his own shoes.

As if responding to what must be incredulous looks from at least a few of us, he backtracks just a bit.

"Of course, the violence that ensued was wrong," he says. "Terribly wrong. I counted both Coach Abrams and his brother Delvin as personal friends, ones I had known for decades, and I still have trouble believing they had any part in any of that. But apparently they did, and Coach Abrams paid for it with his job and then some.

"But the flagrant insubordination that occurred before the violence—and I might add that I believe it *instigated* the violence—was inexcusable and will not be tolerated on this team. The basketball team went nowhere in the playoffs not only because it lost a great coach but also because the team was divided.

"We will not be divided. I won't allow it. There will be no insubordination from petulant, spoiled brats. That's what's wrong with this country these days. I won't allow it. Is that understood?"

His eyes lock on to mine and then Charlie's. Back and forth, like a spectator at a tennis match. Everyone can see him glaring at the two of us. I feel everyone's eyes on me, or at least on me and Charlie.

My ears burn. So does my anger.

I have all I can do to keep it bottled up inside and not let it spew out with the venomous words that are on the tip of my tongue. *What are you, stupid? Ignorant of the facts? Or are you intentionally ignorant? You only want to know the side of the story of your good buddy, Abrams.*

*Or are you as evil as Abrams himself?*

We were not petulant, spoiled brats. What we did was right. What we stood for was justice. We were willing to sacrifice for what we believed in.

Is Dr. Martin Luther King a petulant, spoiled brat? Is it *shenanigans* when he marches in defiance of the institutional bigotry down South? Was his letter from a Birmingham jail insubordination?

"Go ahead, Labelle, say it!" Kowalski taunts, leaning closer, hands on his knees. "It's written all over your face. Spit it out!"

My total lack of a poker face has apparently exposed at least some of what I think about him. I so much want to confirm his suspicions. I want to unleash all the words that are begging to explode from my lips.

But somehow I hold them back. I swallow hard and purse my lips, as if by doing so I lock the words inside.

Kowalski turns to Charlie and appears about to challenge him, too, but holds back.

"You don't have to agree with me," Kowalski says with a look that implies he should win the Nobel Peace Prize for being so magnanimous. He glances back and forth at the two of us. "But I will not have a portion of this team walking out on me. I will not have a portion of this team protesting if I look at one of you cross-eyed."

I feel like my head is about to explode. Comparing what Abrams did to a coach looking at us cross-eyed feels like equating murder with jaywalking.

"There are positions open for some of you freshmen on the JVs and perhaps even one or two on the varsity," Kowalski says. "We got hit pretty hard by graduation from last year's team. And based on Mr. Labelle's exploits on the football field, Charlie Watkins's on the basketball court, and Jessie Stackhouse's in the hockey rink, we have some very talented freshmen athletes. But Labelle and Watkins walked out on their team."

He spits his tobacco juice in my direction. It lands on the ground not more than a foot in front of my black cleats. He fixes his eyes on the two of us again.

"If any of you are thinking you might walk out on this team, I want to know it right now."

I can't hold back any longer.

"Coach, I'll give you everything I've got," I say, trying unsuccessfully to keep my tone calm and even. Instead, my voice shakes with emotion. "No one will work harder."

"That isn't what I said—"

"But I have to be honest. I can't look the other way if you use *that word*—the word Coach Abrams used—to refer to any of my black teammates. If you blatantly discriminate against them because of their color, I'll do what my conscience demands."

Kowalski's eyes widen and his face reddens.

"I guess I was right about you, Labelle," he says. "Enjoy your stay on the freshmen team. You can make your speeches to Coach Gilhooly." Kowalski motions to where Gilhooly stands behind him, looking increasingly uncomfortable, staring at the ground and shifting on his feet. "That is, if he'll even put up with you and doesn't cut your troublemaking ass."

"But as for me," Kowalski says, stabbing himself with his index finger violently in the chest, "I don't care if you hit like Carl Flipping Yastrzemski himself, you'll get to the JVs over my dead body."

*

Mom is waiting for me in her light blue Ford Fairlane, parked on Goodridge Street just outside the half circle that curves toward the front entrance of the school. I toss my books and gym bag in the back seat, and slide in the front. The heater's blowing hot air, which may thaw me out by the time we get home, but probably not.

She has a fried egg sandwich wrapped in wax paper waiting for me. I take it half-heartedly even though I instinctively salivate at the smell. After football and basketball practices, I'd always be ravenous and need something to, as Mom would say, "tide me over" until my father got home from work, usually late, and then we'd eat dinner. But baseball doesn't burn the calories the other sports do, so I'm really only hungry based on our ritual.

I also feel awfully discouraged.

Mom, of course, notices. She can read me like a book. Usually, she first asks how school went to emphasize that my classes are the most important thing and sports comes second, but today she gets right to it.

"What's wrong?" she asks, frowning. "How did it go?"

"Awful," I say, the fried egg sandwich on my lap, still unwrapped inside the wax paper. If I were a little kid, I'd start bawling my eyes out, I feel so upset.

"Really? *Baseball?*" she asks, incredulous. She had shifted the transmission into drive, ready to pull out of the parking spot, but she shifts back into park and stares at me. "You're kidding!"

Mom doesn't know much about sports except for watching me play. She had assumed that when we moved down here to the big, bad city of Lynn, Massachusetts, I'd be as much of a star in every sport as I was up in tiny Plainville, Maine, near the Canadian border, where there are more cows than people. It was a shock to her that being *five-nothin', hundred-nothin'* was a big problem in basketball. I wasn't the next Bob Cousy, and actually struggled just to make the team.

But we both expected baseball to be different. I probably even told her so. In fact, I'm sure I did, setting her expectations as high, or maybe even higher, than mine.

"The coach hates me," I say.

"*What?*" She stares at me, aghast. "*Why?*"

"Because of what happened with the basketball team." I describe how it was just us freshmen, and how he glared at Charlie and me. "He said he wasn't going to put up with any shenanigans like happened on the basketball team."

"Shenanigans? He actually said that?"

"Yeah," I say, and the fury sweeps over me again. "And he said if we were going to walk out on the team, we'd better do it right now."

"You kept quiet, right?" Mom asks, dread in her voice. "You didn't challenge him, did you?"

Now I do stay quiet.

"Oh, Rabbit," she says, and sighs deeply.

# CHAPTER 2

The next morning in front of her locker, my girlfriend, Anna Levesque, tries to offer a ray of hope. She's petite, even shorter than me. Pretty—beautiful, if you ask me—but not in a showy, movie star kind of way. She's quietly pretty, if that makes any sense, with shoulder-length blond hair and soft brown eyes behind maroon-framed glasses. A face that makes you think more of a library than a magazine cover.

But she's the most beautiful girl in the world to me. Smart and sweet. The *best* girl in the world.

And she's *my* girlfriend. She has even told me that she loves me and of course, I've told her I love her, too. But until the night of her chamber quartet's concert a couple weeks ago, we had to hide how we really feel. We had to *imagine* we were holding hands when we'd walk to class together. We had to *imagine* we gave each other a hug. We had to *imagine* we were talking to each other on the phone each night from 7:50 to 8:00. We couldn't write letters to each other.

Even though we loved each other.

All because of the basketball protests. Because of them, her father hated me. He's an ex-Marine who supports the Vietnam War and, according to Anna, thinks those who protest against it are un-American hippies, commies, and cowards who aren't will-ing to fight for their country like he did. And he's as scared as a lot of white people are of Dr. Martin Luther King's protests down

South. Probably scared of almost all black people except Sammy Davis, Jr., Stevie Wonder, and a few athletes.

So when Anna's father saw me in the newspaper and on the TV protesting Coach Abrams' overt racism, he lumped me in with every other protestor that he despises and declared his daughter off-limits. I became pretty much the Devil. Any relationship between Anna and me would be "over his cold, dead body."

Anna couldn't openly defy her parents. She's a good girl, not an apple rotten to the core like me, seemingly at war with everyone despite my best intentions. So we had to pretend. Until the concert.

Anna is an amazing flute player—a flautist—and performs with the school's full orchestra, its eight-piece jazz band, and the city's classical chamber quartet. It makes my jaw drop to listen to her play even though I don't know Bach from Beethoven or Mozart from Mahler. I never even knew that *arpeggio* was a word until I heard it come out of her beautiful mouth.

So nothing can keep me away from her concerts. I wanted to be there for this one even though it was going to include something called "Eight Etudes and a Fantasy for Woodwind Quartet" instead of "Jingle Bells" and "Silent Night" like in her last concert. And I didn't even know what an etude is. You could have said I didn't know an etude from an arpeggio.

Her father's hatred wasn't going to keep me away. Nothing was. And it's not as though I was going to get her into trouble for being there. Friends, even regular friends who are banned from being boyfriends, still go to see their friend's concerts. He couldn't blame her for me being there.

Of course, Anna was wonderful. I was lost with what was happening in a lot of the music. At times it just seemed like a blur of notes. But Anna was great from start to finish, especially when she got a chance to solo. That was my favorite part.

After the concert was over, about twenty parents and friends, myself included, waited in the locker-lined hallway outside the band room to congratulate the quartet members, still inside packing up their instruments and talking to the director, Mr. Wolfe. I saw Anna's parents, and with everyone in a good mood, decided to roll the dice.

I walked over to them, the mother short and blond-haired like Anna, and the father broad-shouldered, with a crew cut befitting an ex-Marine, and with eyes that wanted to burn holes right through me. I had thought a lot about what I might say if given this opportunity, and knew I couldn't talk about principles because mine were different than Anna's father's. Any use of that word would just bury me deeper. I had to talk about loyalty. So before Mr. Levesque could shoot me down, I spoke first.

"I know you don't like me," I said, looking briefly at Anna's mother before turning to her grim-faced father, knowing that he was the problem. "But I wish you'd give me a chance. You might not agree with my participation in the basketball protests, but I sacrificed to remain loyal to my friends. I could have taken the easy way out, become the freshmen team's starting point guard, and let them fight their own battle. But I remained loyal.

"I'd like you to give me the chance to be that loyal to Anna. Let me be the best boyfriend she could ever have."

I could tell from the look on Mrs. Levesque's face that I'd won her over, if I ever had to. But Mr. Levesque just blinked and stared.

Anna spared us the possible stare-down by bursting through the creaking band room door, beautiful in her peach-colored dress and matching bow in her shoulder-length blond hair. She saw me, beamed, and took two running steps before she remembered that we were not supposed to be boyfriend and girlfriend. We were not supposed to be in love. We had to hide what we felt.

She stopped dead in her tracks, still fifteen feet away.

"Hi, Rabbit," she said, trying unsuccessfully to mask the joy on her face. "Thanks for coming."

Either that look on Anna's face or my little speech won the day. That night, Mrs. Levesque convinced her reluctant husband that maybe I wasn't the Devil after all. Anna and I should be allowed to go out. Not actually go out on dates. We're still limited to school functions because we're just fourteen. But we could go out.

No more pretending. No more having to imagine everything from holding hands to talking on the phone with each other.

We were girlfriend and boyfriend again.

*

So today in front of her green-colored locker before school starts, Anna encourages me to fix things with Coach Kowalski like I fixed things with her parents. She's wearing a light yellow sweater and dark slacks that almost match my own while I'm wearing a navy-blue, button-down shirt. The hallways, teeming with other students rushing to their own lockers or heading to homeroom with their books in hand, smell musty, and the air is heavy.

"You got off to a bad start with Coach Kowalski," Anna says. "A horrible start. But if you could get my father to change his mind, you can change *anyone's* mind."

"I don't know," I say doubtfully. "It seemed like Kowalski was trying to provoke Charlie and me. He wanted us to say something. He was like a bully just begging for a fight. Why else would he say that what we did on the basketball team was shenanigans. *Shenanigans!* As if we were just a bunch of troublemakers."

"Well…" Anna says thoughtfully. "It's easy to see how he might view it that way."

"*What?*" If this were anyone but Anna, the word would have come out angry instead of shocked and confused. Easy to see? I can't see it that way *at all*. "We were doing the right thing!"

"Yes, but you have to put yourself in his shoes—"

"I don't want to put myself in his shoes. He's a jerk. And he's wrong about everything!"

A bemused smile comes over Anna's face. It makes her look like an angel, and that softens my anger just a little. But only a little.

"Yes, he was a jerk," she says. "And yes, he was wrong about everything. But look at it from his point of view. He isn't thinking about the justice of your cause on the basketball team. He's thinking about how the problems that developed cost the basketball coach his job. And like you said, Abrams was a friend of his. So he's afraid of that happening to him. He's *afraid* of you and Charlie."

I hadn't looked at it that way. But just thinking of the word *shenanigans* still makes my blood boil. I feel like my head is about to explode. I don't want to put my feet in his disgusting shoes.

"He has the power to ruin your season if he wants to," Anna says. "It's important you fix things so he doesn't hold it against you the rest of the season. Maybe even for every baseball season into the future. Make it clear that you really aren't a threat at all, just like you convinced my parents that you weren't a threat to me. Convince Kowalski that you're a great teammate. You don't want problems any more than he does. You want to help the team."

I look into those soft brown eyes of Anna's that could make me promise to climb Mt. Everest. I hear what she's saying, but it sounds too easy. Too simple. Maybe with someone else, but not Coach Kowalski.

"I'm not sure if there's any communicating with him," I say. "He hates me and nothing I say is going to change that."

"Maybe you're right," Anna says, nodding. "But you could have said the same thing about my father."

I shrug, filled with doubt, and the homeroom bell rings.

*Yikes!* Time flies when I'm with Anna. She gives me a quick hug, but it's long enough for me to drink in the pleasing lilac scent of her perfume. I smile.

Together, we sprint for homeroom.

*

Later that morning, I spot Charlie in the bustling hallways between class, walking in the other direction with Jamaal. Charlie and I also played football together, but Jamaal only plays basketball. No football, no baseball.

I give them both a nod and a smile. I'm alone because Anna and I don't share this next class, and my former best friends with whom I share I share most classes, Jeff Goodwin and Paul DiSimone, turned their backs on me during the basketball protests. They decided I was a traitor to the white race, or at least that I ruined the basketball season, so I don't walk with them anymore. Good riddance to bad rubbish, as my mom would say.

Charlie motions me over. Jamaal is shorter and thinner than Charlie—about halfway between my five-one and Charlie's five-nine—but even blacker than Charlie. They're both wearing dark slacks and button-down shirts. We cluster up against the green lockers.

"Hey, didn't get a chance to talk to you after practice," Charlie says. "Appreciate what you said, man, but maybe we need to just lay low. Hold our tongues, you know? We already got targets on our backs."

His words take me back. "You think I was wrong?"

"No, no, you was right. Hundred percent. Just seems like…I don't know…like the more we talk, the worse it get."

My ears burn. "I got a big mouth."

"You right about that," Jamaal says.

"I actually was gonna try to talk to Kowalski before practice today," I say, deciding to keep to myself that this is Anna's idea. "Clear the air, you know?"

Charlie winces, but says nothing.

"The boy do like to talk," Jamaal says.

"Who you callin' boy?" I say, and we laugh.

*

I sprint from my last class to the gym locker room, get dressed in record time, and race outside. My cleats click on the asphalt parking lot between the school and the field. Exhaust fumes fill the air even though by now the lot is mostly empty; only a half dozen cars remain. I'm hoping to talk to Coach Kowalski before practice, and I luck out. I'm the first kid onto the field, but the four coaches are all there talking beside the metal backstop at the varsity field.

I don't want to interrupt so I stand there politely, hanging back out of earshot so I don't intrude on their conversation. It isn't as cold as yesterday, but even so, I shiver. I've mentally rehearsed my speech, but that doesn't make me any less nervous. A bitter taste forms in my mouth.

"Move along to the freshman field," Kowalski says dryly.

"Coach, if I could have just one minute of your—"

"I said move along, *Rebel*," he says, announcing the word as if I've got a new nickname. Coach Gilhooly, the freshmen team coach, looks away as does JV Coach Fitzgerald, but Kowalski's stocky varsity assistant, Coach Particelli, snickers. "To the freshmen field where you belong."

"Yes, sir," I say, "But if you'll just give me a chance—"

"You had your chance yesterday, Labelle." Kowalski's face is hard as stone. "Give your rebel speeches on the freshmen field. Move along or I'll cut your spoiled brat ass right now."

My heart sinks. Kowalski isn't going to change his mind. Not now. Not ever. He isn't even going to give me a chance to change it.

Certainly not this year. Maybe never. Next year, even if I've hit over .500 with a stolen base in every attempt on the freshmen team, he'll make the same speech, then taunt me to bury myself yet again.

And I probably will.

So I decide to go down fighting. I start walking toward the freshmen field—toward baseball oblivion—but I don't do so quietly.

"I can help this team win, maybe even the varsity," I say, looking at Kowalski as I walk. "I *want* to help this team win. I'm a team player." I slow down, but keep moving. "I'll *never* be a problem." I pause just a second, then resume putting one foot slowly after another, craning my neck to look back. "Not unless you're Lynn's version of George Wallace and Bull Connor, and prove it by your actions. And I don't think you're like that at all."

This part may be wishful thinking. For all I know, he's planning to cast his presidential vote for Wallace, the Georgia segregationist.

For all I know, Kowalski admires Bull Connor, the racist head of the Birmingham, Alabama, police, who unleashed attack dogs and fire hoses on those who were peacefully protesting discrimination with Dr. King. For all I know, Kowalski thinks the N-word every time he looks at a black person. After all, he considered Abrams a friend, and thinks we troublemakers, we *rebels*, provoked the whole thing.

But I have to hope, even if it's a long shot, that he's a reasonable man. Or at least has *one* reasonable bone in his body. Surely, he has to realize that his taunting practically forced me to speak up yesterday.

"I think you're a good man," I say, raising the volume to be sure this part of my message isn't missed. I switch from craning my neck backwards to turning around to face Kowalski and walking backwards. "A good man who just doesn't want to suffer the same fate as Coach Abrams. Unless you're like George Wallace and Bull Connor, you won't."

"The kid never shuts up," Kowalski says in amazement to the other coaches, shaking his head. "He's worse than my wife!"

They laugh.

"I want the same thing you want," I say, spreading my hands wide. "I just want to play baseball. That's all. I don't want trouble any more than you do. Just baseball."

I begin to wonder if I've gotten through. Could it be? I slow down almost to a stop.

But then Kowalski's stony face returns, and he bellows, "Move along, Rebel!" As if to emphasize his point, he spits a stream of tobacco juice in my general direction. It only goes a few feet, but I get the point.

I turn and make the long walk to the freshman field.

That went well.

*

There's a little extra pop in my warm-up throws with "Moose" Mahoney, who's wearing a catcher's mitt. Moose is huge, though not really that tall. He was an offensive tackle on the JV football team, an admittedly flabby two hundred and ten pounds then and even heavier now. Once, after I scored a touchdown, he lifted me up onto his shoulders like I weighed little more than a couple of cheeseburgers.

For some reason, he seemed hesitant to pair off with me today, giving a shrug and saying, "I guess so." It seemed an odd response. He didn't play basketball, and we don't go to any of the same classes, so our last shared memory was joyfully whooping it up after the big win over our cross-town rival, Lynn Classical.

Good times.

By the time Charlie and Jessie arrive together, I've convinced myself that Moose's reluctance was all in my head. Turns out, I'm wrong about that, but it'll be batting practice before I find out for sure.

"You say anything to Kowalski?" Charlie asks, standing next to me as Jessie grabs a ball out of the pea-green duffle bag with LEHS scribbled on the side in faded black marker.

I nod somberly, and Charlie winces. "Didn't go well?"

I shake my head.

"Not gonna say, 'I told you so,'" he says, catching a toss from Jessie, who's standing thirty feet away, next to Moose.

"But you told me so," I say, finishing the line for him.

"Man, the way you run your mouth off," Charlie says, shaking his head. "Lots of places—and not just down South—if you were black, you'd be dead."

I start to give a small laugh, but Charlie ain't laughing. So I just nod, and with a sinking feeling, I realize he's right. With nothing intelligent to say, I for once keep my big trap shut.

*

Half an hour later, I step to the plate for my turn at batting practice, the protective dark blue helmet square on my head, the Louisville Slugger comfortable in my hands. Coach Gilhooly is pitching, tufts of brown hair poking out from beneath his gray-with-maroon-letters LEHS cap. Behind the plate squats Moose

Mahoney, his catcher's mitt now augmented by a dusty, navy-blue chest protector, black shin guards, and a black metal catcher's mask.

He doesn't even wait for the first pitch.

"If it ain't the white Martin Luther King," Moose says, his words slightly muffled coming from behind his catcher's mask. "Nice speech yesterday!"

I'm stunned. I had thought Moose was my friend. What happened to the guy who carried me on his shoulders after I scored the big touchdown?

I guess I should have known. I learned during the basketball season that you can go from being a hero to the object of hatred and derision in close to zero seconds flat.

"Thank you!" I say, playing dumb to Moose's sarcasm.

Coach Gilhooly's first pitch comes down the middle of the plate. A meatball.

*Crack!*

I send it rocketing into the left-centerfield alley. A double or maybe even a triple in a game.

"I didn't mean that as a compliment," Moose says from behind the plate.

"I know," I say, getting ready for the next pitch, my knees slightly bent, legs apart slightly more than shoulder's width.

The pitch comes in. Not a meatball, a good pitch on the inside corner at the knees. But I turn on it, and get full leg drive. *Crack!* A frozen rope over the third baseman's head, down the line, past the left fielder. Another double.

In the cold, the bat stings in my hands, but it's a good sting. It feels great.

"If I ever make one-millionth the difference in this world as Dr. King," I say, trying to speak softly so only the knucklehead behind the plate can hear it, no one else, "I'll be a happy man."

"You sure you ain't black?" Moose says.

"You sure you ain't a moron?" I reply.

The next pitch comes in on the outside corner. *Crack!* Into the right-center alley.

Three pitches. Three doubles or triples. Can't do much better than that.

But I see a look of displeasure on Coach Gilhooly's face. I belatedly realize that he must have heard what I just said to Moose. Not long after promising what a great team player I'll be. Words that probably ring hollow for Coach Gilhooly now. Moose deserved what I said to him, but he'll get no more from me. It's time for me to zip it shut and live up to my promise to the coaches.

So when Moose says something else, I don't even register the words. I've tuned him out.

I'm going to be a great teammate. Even to a knucklehead like Moose.

*Crack!*

*Crack!*

*Crack!*

I'm letting my bat do the talking.

And when Dennis Martel, a freckle-faced redhead who's trying out as a pitcher and has been warming up, comes in to replace Coach Gilhooly, the bat keeps talking.

*Crack!*

*Crack!*

*Crack!*

I hold my tongue even when the next pitch comes in at my head. I hit the dirt, and when Moose laughs, as if he called for the beanball—and for all I know, maybe he did—I don't say a thing.

*Crack!*

*Crack!*

*Crack!*

# CHAPTER 3

My father hits the roof when he hears the news about me and the baseball team. We're seated at the dinner table, he at the head of the table to my left, still wearing his black suit and tightly-knotted dark blue tie. My mother is at the other end in her brown dress. I'm in the middle, still wearing my school clothes. In better times, back up in Maine, I joked that this is a Rabbit sandwich. But those days seem long gone.

Behind me, the wall clock audibly ticks—*tick…tick…tick*—and I face the kitchen, from which Mom and I have carried a platter of steaming meatloaf, a big bowl of mashed potatoes, a smaller bowl of buttered peas, and what Mom calls a gravy boat filled with thick, brown gravy.

All my father has carried to the table is his attitude.

It's been cold, hostile, and distant since the basketball protests. It had been bad before that, but it got a lot worse when Mom wouldn't do as he ordered. She didn't just participate in the protest, she made the placards we held and contacted the newspapers and TV stations to create the publicity we needed.

My father went from mortified and bewildered to furious and defeated. A cold fury remains, an icy wall that divides him from us, even as he seems eaten from the inside by resentment that we would *defy* his authority and make him look bad at work.

Him and his *job*.

It's a job for which he'd happily sell his soul to the Devil just to get the next promotion, and then the next one after that. It was a promotion that made him drag me away from my friends and the peaceful happiness in Plainfield, Maine, where the worst thing that ever seemed to happen was the smell of manure in the fields, down here to this armpit of a city. "Lynn, Lynn, City of Sin, never come out, the way you went in," the saying goes. He and I have feuded almost constantly since.

I suppose it isn't a total armpit of a city. That isn't fair. There are some good things about living here in the big, bad city. Especially Anna. In many ways, she cancels out everything I hate about being down here. And I also had some great times on the football field, which wasn't possible in Plainfield, where not even the regional high school had enough boys to field a team.

There are admittedly neat things about the city. Like Lynn Woods, which has miles and miles of wooded area for hiking, more than in almost any other city in America. And there's the waterfront, although the only time I was down there it stank of rotting seaweed. Jeff Goodwin, back when he was my friend before the protests showed me his true colors, said it isn't rotting seaweed, it's backed-up sewage, which is just about the most disgusting thing I can think of. Of course, Jeff makes up all kinds of things, so I don't believe him for a second. I might hate this city sometimes, but I don't hate it *that* much.

Things sure got a lot more complicated down here, though. I've had a lot more problems. I never got sucker-punched or had my lunch money taken away from me before we moved here. I never had a Hells Angel point a gun to my head. I never had a psycho like Jimmy Keenan attack me with a baseball bat. Twice, once during the football season because I was taking his starting position on the team, and once as part of Delvin Abrams' gang of thugs, attacking us during the basketball protests.

And who's the reason I've had to endure those things? Who's the reason I'm down here and not back in Plainfield? *Dear old Dad.*

I guess he doesn't have a monopoly on bad attitudes. In a lot of ways, we're like America and the Russians. We don't like each other. We don't trust each other. And we've got the nuclear warheads poised to strike. The threat of Mutually Assured Destruction—both sides obliterate each other in a cloud of nuclear dust—hangs heavy in the air between us.

Of course, he's the Russians; I'm the good guys. Although I'm sure he thinks the same thing.

Two bad attitudes just waiting to explode and blow each other to bits.

He explodes now after hearing about my confrontation with Coach Kowalski. I've managed to eat three bites of juicy meatloaf and two bites of mashed potatoes swimming in gravy, feeling like a prisoner awaiting his firing squad. The shots would have been fired the night before had my father actually eaten dinner with Mom and me, but he worked until almost ten o'clock, so I got a twenty-four hour reprieve. And I got those bites of meatloaf and mashed potatoes because it took my father that long to break his stony silence and actually say something to me.

"So how are baseball tryouts going?" he asks, his face blank and without emotion or any indication of true interest. Like a stranger commenting on the weather just to break a silence that has become too awkward to leave alone.

"Okay," I say, and glance at my mother, who purses her lips.

She hates arguments at the dinner table. Of course, she hates arguments any time and any place. In fact, when she came up to my bedroom last night to tell me my father had finally gotten home, and instructed me to go downstairs to wish him good night, she specifically told me not to say anything about Coach Kowalski because it was too late to start an argument. As if the time of day has ever stopped my father and me from having an argument. But she hates arguments at the dinner table most of all.

So I just add, "I was killing the ball during batting practice."

"Good," my father says, a slight thawing apparent in his voice. "What team? JV? Varsity?"

I glance at Mom, who just looks down at her food. She knows we're not going to make it through this meal peacefully.

"Freshmen," I say.

"In baseball? Really?" He frowns. "I know we underestimated the size factor in basketball, but you've always starred in baseball. Size shouldn't be holding you back there. There isn't a pitcher who can throw a fastball past you."

I swallow hard. "It's only the second day of tryouts." I take a deep breath. "None of the freshmen have moved up yet, not even Charlie and Jessie, and they're hitting rocket shots in BP. In batting practice."

"The two Negroes?"

I roll my eyes. I can't help it. It is so like him to make that comment, to view them as nothing more than members of their race.

He sees my reaction and isn't happy about it. Something flares in his eyes. He stabs his index finger against the middle of his black-rimmed glasses frame, pushing it so hard against the bridge of his nose I wonder if he'll have a bruise there tomorrow.

"*What?*" he says, and gestures with his free hand that isn't holding his fork. "I didn't call them *colored* or any of the really bad words. What's wrong with what I said?"

"First off, they prefer the term *black*," I say.

My father's fork clatters to his plate. "For crying out loud, they can't make up their minds what they want to be called."

"Secondly," I say, plowing straight ahead, "you could have just called them my friends. Charlie is my best friend, and Jessie isn't far behind. That's what you should think of first about them, not their race."

My father glares at me with a look of pure hatred.

"Don't you lecture me, young man! I am sick and tired of your know-it-all attitude. You might want to do a whole lot less talking and a lot more listening."

I hold my tongue, although there's plenty I feel like saying. But if he wants to muzzle me, *fine*! I'll happily go the rest of my life without wasting a word on him. As long as I don't have to listen to any of *his* nonsense.

I shovel a big chunk of meatloaf into my mouth. Somehow, it doesn't taste quite as juicy as before, and the spices that made it so delicious before are no longer doing the trick.

I glance at Mom. Her shoulders slump. She's admitting defeat in her quest for a peaceful family dinner. Then she waves the white flag of surrender. "Let's get it over with, Rabbit," she says, the resignation clear in her voice. "Tell him about you and Coach Kowalski."

I take a long time finishing that big bite of meatloaf before I swallow it. Longer than I really need. I point to my mouth as chew after chew grinds the meat down into a pulp. All the while, my father gives me an exasperated look that borders on anger. It all but screams *I can't believe you're in trouble again. You are such a rotten kid.*

When I can't stall any longer, I say, "I may be with the freshmen team a while."

"And why is that? What happened between you and the coach?"

I swallow hard, then tell my father. With every sentence, every attempt to explain why I couldn't remain silent, his face clouds over with more and more anger. He waits until I finish before he explodes.

To my shock, he turns to Mom and points a finger at her.

"I hope you're happy now!" he says. Mom's eyes widen. He gestures with disgust in my direction. "Look at the *monster* you've created!"

"He is not—"

"He's a monster with no respect at all for authority. He thinks he can mouth off to anyone, *and it's all your fault*!"

Mom's eyes well with tears, which then spill down her cheeks, but my father doesn't slow down a beat. In fact, it's almost as if he gains strength seeing her cry.

"You've coddled him ever since we got here," he says in almost a shout, a small bit of spittle flying out of his mouth. "You've allowed him to be disrespectful to both of us. He's deserved a good beating, but you've always stepped in and taken his side. Spare the rod and spoil the child. Well, you've spoiled this brat but good. And now the whole world can see what your permissive attitudes have created. You've turned him into a monster!"

I can't believe what I'm hearing. Not because I care what my father—the true monster in the room—is saying. He could call me a baboon's butt, for all I care. His opinion means nothing to me. He's a jerk and a moron.

But his attack on my mom has taken my breath away. I can't swallow. I can't move. I watch the tears flowing down her face, and I want to kill him. Not actually murder him, of course, but I want to hurt him for hurting the most wonderful mom a son could hope for.

"Stop it!" I finally shout, leaning forward toward my father, his face now almost purple with rage. "Leave her alone!"

He winds up and backhands me across the face so hard I topple off the chair and onto the floor. I land on my knees, then rock over onto my rear end. I hear my mother scream, but it feels like from far in the distance. I see stars. The bitter taste of what must be blood fills my mouth.

My father has slapped me before, but never this hard, never with the back of his hand. His hard knuckles make a better weapon than the fleshy part of the palm. Perhaps I was just off balance, leaning forward like I was in my seat, but he still hit me so hard he knocked me to the ground.

That's never happened before.

I don't ever want it to happen again, but I'd rather take this than see the pain in my mother's eyes as he tells her she's created a monster—*me*. I'd rather take this than see those tears streak down her face.

I realize her screams have given way to words.

"If you lay one more hand on him, I will leave you this minute!" she says, her voice shaking. She's standing, so I can see her from where I sit on the floor. I can't see her palms, but she seems to be leaning on them, placed on the table, for support.

"Spare the rod, spoil the child!" my father yells back.

"I will leave you," she says, "and I won't come back."

"You played that card once before," my father says, saying out loud what I guessed months ago, and Mom inadvertently confirmed. She'd told me it had to remain our secret. My father couldn't know that I knew she had threatened him this way. He wouldn't be able to handle knowing that I knew.

But now he's spilled the beans. He doesn't seem to have realized it, however. He keeps right on going. "Now look at the result. I hope you're happy!"

"I am *so* happy with Rabbit! He's a wonderful kid! I'm *disgusted* with you!"

My father moves toward her. Her eyes widen in panic. She backs up.

Belatedly, I scramble to my feet, crashing against the chair, ready to lunge across the table at him to protect her. But I know I'm too late. Way too late.

My legs feel unsteady beneath me. I wobble.

All I have is my mouth. My big mouth that has caused so much trouble. But it's all I've got now.

"Don't you dare touch her!" I shout. "If you do—"

But I don't need to complete the threat. He brushes past Mom, glances back at me, and with total disdain says, "I wasn't going to lay a hand on her. You're the only one that needs a beating."

He stomps out the front door, slamming it behind him, and drives off down the street.

Mom rushes over to check my face, and asks if I'm all right. Words fail me. All I can do is nod.

And then as she wraps her arms around me, I lose it. Uncontrollable, wracking sobs take over me, gushing out like a river. My body shakes. I taste warm, salty tears mixed with blood on my lips. Snot runs down my nose. Like I'm a pathetic little baby.

Mom tries to console me with words I barely hear. I want to console her. After all, my father attacked her with words more vicious than the backhanded slap he delivered to me, but I can't manage even a single word. My throat feels like a clenched fist. I can barely swallow.

I want to say something, but I can't.

Then I realize that she's crying, too. Her body shakes, too, over-come with horrible, wracking sobs that make me cry all the harder.

*

I'm not sure how long we stand like that, arms wrapped around each other, each of our sobs feeding the other's. It feels like a very long time.

But finally, we're cried out. There are no more tears, no more uncontrollable sobs left in us.

We're spent.

I go to clean off my face in the bathroom, but Mom stops me. She puts her hands on my shoulders, holding me at arm's length, and her eyes lock on to mine.

"You need to know something," she says, her voice shaking with emotion. "You are not a monster. You are a wonderful, caring young man with more principles and integrity than that…than that…" She takes a deep breath, and grips my shoulders tightly. "Than anyone else I know. Do you know that?"

I shrug. It's a wonderful thing she's just said, but I don't believe it. Me and my big mouth have created this whole mess. This is really all my fault. Maybe I am just a spoiled brat. Maybe I deserved to get smacked across the face. Maybe I better get used to the bitter taste of blood in my mouth. Maybe sparing the rod—whatever the rod is supposed to mean—has spoiled this child.

But even if I'm as bad as my father says, even if I am a monster, it isn't Mom's fault. It's mine.

"I'm sorry," I say with a catch in my voice that if I weren't already all cried out might send me back over that edge. "I know I have a big mouth. It's just—"

"Listen to me, young man," Mom says. "Nobody is perfect. You may need to learn that there are times to speak up and times to be quiet." She forces a grin. "Not even Dr. King can say *everything* that comes to his mind."

The scary thing is that I don't say everything that comes to my mind either. I actually do hold back sometimes. But I still open my big yap so much more than I ought to. It still is always getting me in trouble.

"But your heart is always in the right place," Mom continues. "You've got such a big heart, and sometimes that big heart all but forces you to speak up." She grins and shakes my shoulders playfully. "Sometimes it's that thick skull of yours. And you do have a bit of a rebellious streak in you at times. In those cases, you do need to be quiet. But you'll learn. It's part of growing up. And the big thing is to keep your heart in the right place."

She touches a palm to my chest. I nod. I suppose it'll get easier to keep quiet when I get older. I sure hope it does.

"I feel bad," I begin, hoping that she doesn't cut me off again or my throat doesn't close up so I can barely speak. "I feel bad that he said all those awful things about you." My father has become just *he*. He isn't *Dad* anymore. He hasn't been *Dad* for a while, and certainly not now. He isn't worthy of that word. He's just *he*. "He blamed you for what I've become, but it isn't your fault. He said it was all your fault, but it isn't. It's my fault."

"Listen to me," Mom says, and grips my shoulders so hard it almost hurts. "He said that you are all my fault, but I don't see it that way at all. If he wants to admit that he hasn't been much of a father since we moved down here, then I'll accept that. I'll agree with that. But that doesn't mean you are all my fault.

"That means I get all the *credit* for what a wonderful person you are. I'm *proud* of you, even if your mouth runs away from you at times. I am *so* proud. There's no blame to accept. I'll take the *credit*."

My jaw drops. I swallow hard.

"You…are…wonderful," she says. "Now I want to hear you say it. Say 'I'm wonderful.' I want to hear it."

I just stare at her, still trying to fully appreciate what she has just said.

"Say 'I'm wonderful,'" she says again.

I swallow hard, then eke out a weak grin. "You're wonderful."

We both laugh.

"I mean it," she says.

So I say it.

I'm not sure I believe it. In fact, I'm sure I don't believe it. But it does make me feel better to say the words.

"You need to say it, too," I say.

Mom blinks. She forces a tight grin, then repeats my joke. "You're wonderful."

"Say it!"

She does, and I feel just a little bit better.

# CHAPTER 4

I wake up the next morning with a black eye.

I stare into the bathroom mirror. I can't believe what I'm seeing. My eyes widen. My jaw drops. I'm standing there at the white porcelain sink in my school clothes, the smell of deodorant in the air, my blue toothbrush in my hand with a smear of white toothpaste on its bristles, and the mint taste of the toothpaste in my mouth. Just like it's any other weekday.

But it's suddenly not just any other weekday.

The black eye is faint, the grayish color of charcoal briquettes after they've burned through, and only a thin curving line beneath the eye, maybe only half an inch thick. Nowhere near as bad as the one Smitty gave me on the bus my first week of school here when I wouldn't give him my lunch money. That shiner was a really ugly one, an almost neon-bright purple and black, baseball-sized as if a fastball had hit me flush in the eye like Tony Conigliaro. Smitty got me pretty good.

This one is nothing like that. But it's unmistakably still a black eye. And everyone is going to see it.

An icy chill runs down my back as my shock gives way to panic.

*What am I going to say? How can I possibly explain this?*

I taste something foul in my mouth. I'm going to get asked a hundred times today who hit me. Maybe even two or three hundred. I'm sure not going to admit that my father belted me at the dinner table. Hit me so hard he knocked me on the floor. That would be humiliating.

*But what else can I say?*

I suddenly feel nauseous and a bit lightheaded. This isn't at all like with Smitty, which was plenty embarrassing. Nothing like that had ever happened to me before. Nothing like that happened at all up in Plainfield, Maine. So sure, it was embarrassing. It's never a proud moment when you get the stuffing knocked out of you. But Smitty is a tough guy, a senior, a goon who fortunately is no longer part of my life, but has beaten up plenty of kids like me.

*But my father?*

I can't admit that my father did this to me. Everyone gets the belt to their behind every now and then, I suppose, some of us more than others, but a black eye? What will my classmates think? What about my teachers?

Then a truly chilling thought hits me.

*What will Anna think?*

Last night on the phone, I told her that my father and I had argued, and he predictably blamed me for the problems with Coach Kowalski, but I couldn't tell her that he'd hit me so hard he knocked me off my chair.

I just couldn't say that. Couldn't admit it.

Just like I couldn't also tell her that he called me a monster, and it was all my mother's fault. I always want to be honest with Anna, and she knows I argue with my father all the time. He even banned Anna and me from talking on the phone for a while a few months back. So she knows there are problems.

But if I admit that he's called me a monster, what might that make her think about me? And it's one thing to argue with your parents. It's another to get whacked so hard you get knocked to the ground and you wake up the next day with a black eye, even one that isn't all that bad as black eyes go.

*What am I going to say to Anna now?*

I'll have to admit that I wasn't totally truthful with her last night. I didn't lie to her on the phone, but it was, I suppose, a fib of omission. *Oh, yeah, I forgot to tell you that my father hit me pretty hard. I meant to tell you, but it just...slipped my mind. I just forgot.*

My heart sinks as I consider how I'm going to tell her. Who cares what everyone else thinks? Who cares if they call me "raccoon eyes" even if it's only the one eye, and pretty faint at that?

*But what is Anna going to think?*

I hear the stairs creak heavily. My father, the Devil himself, is walking downstairs. Anger wells up within me. *He's* the one who has done this to me. It's *his* fault I'm now wracking my brain, trying to think of what I'll say to Anna. It's *his* fault I'm going to have everyone else at school asking what happened to me, and I'll need some excuse because I can't let anyone know that *he's* the one who gave me this black eye.

I set my toothbrush on the back of the sink next to the cold water faucet, the remnants of the toothpaste still on its bristles, and rush downstairs. I'll come back to finish brushing my teeth and getting ready for school later. But I don't want my father, the real monster in this house, to escape without seeing what he did. He may be robotically walking out the door, ignoring my mother's offer of at least coffee, like he does when he's really furious with us, when he's trying to totally shut us out of his life.

If so, I'll race out to his car, and if he's already inside, bang on the window and then point to what he's done. He's going to see it.

*And a good morning to you, dear old Dad!*

But I don't need to chase after him. He's sliding into his accustomed seat at the head of the dining room table, a steaming cup of coffee in one hand and the *Boston Globe* in the other. Both were handed to him, I'm sure, by my mother, who's back at the stove now, turned away from us. She's cooking bacon and eggs that are sizzling in the frying pan, the kitchen separated from the dining room by only a countertop. The smells fill the air, and despite my rage, my mouth instinctively salivates.

My father slurps loudly at his coffee and sets it down on the table. He glances at me with a look of disdain, then lifts the front page of the *Globe*, burying his face in the news.

*He didn't even see my black eye. Didn't even see it!*

I can't believe it. How do you look at your own son, even with such a fleeting glance filled with hatred and disgust, and fail to notice his black eye? Of course, he was really looking right *through* me, as if I were transparent, or not even really there.

To him, I might as well be invisible.

"Morning, Rabbit!" Mom calls out over her shoulder from the stove. "I'll have your eggs and bacon in a second. Get some orange juice out of the refrigerator, will you?"

I walk into the kitchen, and stand next to her, my body turned to face her square on. She flips the bacon, sizzling and popping, with a metal spatula, and brushes her hand against her white apron. She glances over, a slight smile on her face.

She shrieks.

The spatula clatters to the stovetop. She cups my face in her hands and stares wide-eyed at me.

"Will you look at this!" she shouts at my father. She takes my hand and pulls me toward the dining room until we're standing at the opposite end of the table. My father has lowered the newspaper. Behind us, a piece of bacon snaps. Mom points at my eye.

"Look at what you've done!" she shouts, all but screaming. "I hope you're happy!"

He stares at me blankly, then frowns. "What happened?"

*What happened? What does he think happened?*

"*You* happened!" my mother yells, squeezing my hand so tightly it hurts. "You hit Rabbit so hard you knocked him off the chair, for crying out loud. Knocked him to the ground! What do you think happened? I hope you're proud of yourself!"

"It was just…." Bewilderment and concern flash across my father's face. "He must have fallen down—"

"You *knocked* him down!"

"—or he got hit by a baseball. I only—"

"He didn't get hit by a baseball. He got hit by a pathetic excuse for a father!"

All the blood drains from my father's face.

"You *used* to be a good father," Mom says. "But now, look at what you've done!" She points to the black eye.

"But…but he…" my father sputters. "He used to be a good kid."

"He is still a good kid! In fact, he's a *great* kid. A son you should be proud of."

My father shrinks back from the words, as if *he's* been slapped. His face, pale white moments ago, flushes with anger. Fire sparks in his eyes.

"He shows no respect for authority," he says. "And whose fault is that? Yours! He mouths off at the drop of a hat. And whose fault is that? Yours! He's become a spoiled brat. And whose fault is that? Yours!"

My father stands, crumpling the section of the newspaper he'd been reading into a ball. He slams it onto the table, where it takes two hops and topples onto the floor.

"We've got a monster on our hands, thanks to you," he shouts, his face flushed. He leans close, his palms flat on the table for support. "Now *I've* got to fix it. Well, if I've got to slap some sense into him, then I'll do it!"

"If you hit Rabbit like that again," my mother says, her voice suddenly soft, almost a whisper, but firm, "it will be the last thing you do."

*

My heart is in my throat as I walk to Anna's locker, trying to rehearse what I'm going to say.

After my father stormed out, Mom applied some makeup to try to hide the discoloration about my eye. I objected at first, horrified at the very thought of wearing makeup, the most girly thing imaginable, but Mom insisted even though she rarely wears makeup herself. She said it was just something called "foundation," whatever that is, and that actors and men on TV wear it all the time. It wasn't as if, she said, she was applying lipstick and mascara, which was the real girly stuff, although if I wanted to give that a try, I should let her know. That made both of us laugh, even though we really weren't in much of a laughing mood.

Seems like she was right. The "foundation" seems to be working. The school's bustling hallways are filled with conversation and laughter, but none of it is directed at me. No one points at me and grins. No one asks who hit me. No one calls me a one-eyed raccoon. I just walk along, smelling the cigarette smoke billowing out of the boys room when the door opens as I walk past it. I keep my head down, holding my two textbooks by my side, instead of looking for friends I can nod to.

As I near Anna's locker, I look up, and see her coming to meet me, a beaming smile on her face. She's wearing a peach-colored dress, beautiful as ever, and despite my nerves, I can't help but respond to her radiant, thousand-watt smile. I smile even though my heart is in my throat.

Until she stops about ten feet away. *Uh-oh.* I stop, too.

Anna cocks her head and looks at me strangely. Her eyes scrunch up in a confused look.

"Rabbit," she asks slowly. "Are you wearing…makeup?"

I want to die.

"Is that…" she begins, and then a pained look comes to her eyes. "Are you covering up a black eye?"

My heart sinks. My shoulders slump. A lump the size of Massachusetts forms in my throat.

I shrug. "Kind of."

"What happened?"

I'm prepared to tell anyone else that it happened on the baseball field. I'll even elaborate with the half-truth that Dennis Martel threw a beanball at me, and I might even speculate that Moose Mahoney was behind it all. With everyone else, I'll use the baseball excuse that my jerk of a father gave me while trying to deny his own guilt.

Talk about doubling up on a lie.

But I can't lie to Anna.

I so badly want to hide the truth—the shameful, humiliating truth that makes me feel so small and worthless—but I care for her too much, I *love* her too much!—to lie to her even when the truth is so ugly.

"You've got to swear you won't tell anyone else," I say, my voice and hands shaking with emotion.

"Of course, Rabbit," Anna says. She takes my hand, and leads me to her locker. With a soft voice and tenderness in the brown eyes behind her glasses, she says, "Tell me."

I draw in a deep breath, and let a pack of students go past us.

"I'm going to tell everyone else that it happened on the baseball field yesterday. I don't want anyone else to know what really happened."

She nods.

"I don't really want you to know, either," I admit.

"You don't have to tell me if you don't want to," Anna says. "But I think you need to get it off your chest." She bites her lower lip. "I want to help you."

I almost burst into tears. That's how much of a baby I am. It was just a little slap, I tell myself. Not even a punch. Just a slap, when I probably deserved a beating. I've been making such a big deal out of it, but the only person who has even spotted the foundation-covered black eye is Anna.

I'm *such* a baby.

But what makes me want to cry, what fills me with such shame and sadness and a feeling of such utter worthlessness, is that look of hatred and disgust by my father.

I'm such a monster.

The same father who, little more than six months ago, played catch with me in the backyard, and cheered me on during my baseball and basketball games, and laughed with me and…

…and *loved* me.

And was *proud* of me.

Now, he *hates* me. I *disgust* him.

To him, I'm a *monster*.

That's what hurts so bad. Not the physical pain of that back-handed slap. If that slap had been delivered by a stranger, I would have already forgotten about it. It certainly wasn't pleasant, but it didn't hurt *that* bad. My face stung, and I tasted blood for a short while, and I've got the faintest of black eyes now.

But none of that matters.

It's what that slap did to my heart.

It's what that slap means.

I'm a disgusting monster who needs the Devil beat out of me.

"Rabbit?" Anna asks. "We can talk about it later, if that's what you need. But I think we should talk about it sometime."

"My father hit me," I say, all but spitting it out. "Hit me so hard he knocked me off the chair and onto the floor."

The rest all comes out in a torrent of emotion and anger and hurt until finally there's nothing more to say. Anna just holds me in her arms. I drink in the smell of strawberries in her hair and wonder what she could possibly see in a monster like me.

# CHAPTER 5

That night, just before bedtime, Mom steps inside my bedroom doorframe. She leans against it, wearing her white bathrobe, and crosses her arms. I'm sitting on my bed on top of the covers, my back leaning on a pillow propped up against the headboard. I've changed into my Boston Red Sox pajamas, navy blue with bright red lettering. It's a modest sized room with a window and small closet on my right, a nightstand and dark brown dresser on my left, and a matching desk and chair straight ahead, past the foot of the bed, up against the wall. Color posters of Tony Conigliaro, Rico Petrocelli, and of course, Carl Yastrzemski—each of them in mid-swing—fill the spare wall space.

I've been listening to a cassette tape of one of Anna's concerts, hoping it will cheer me up. It almost always makes me happy, especially hearing one of her solos, but not tonight. I just can't concentrate on the music.

All I can think about is my father hitting me. Knocking me onto the floor. Making it so I have to wear makeup when I go to school to cover up my black eye. *Makeup!* The black eye is faint. Barely visible. But it's there. And I'm sure it's going to get worse.

I hate him.

I hate myself, too, because I'm the one who made him do it. Me and my big mouth started the whole thing. I may have been trying to defend Mom when he gave me the backhanded slap, but

I got the whole thing started. If I weren't such a rotten kid, such a spoiled brat, *such a monster*, he wouldn't have to hit me.

I've been dreading Mom coming up here, telling me I need to go downstairs and say goodnight to him. I really don't want to face him. Can't face him. He wasn't home by 8:30, so we went ahead and ate dinner by ourselves. Mom asked for the billionth time if my eye was okay, and did any teachers ask about it, and I reassured her that it was fine and they didn't. Since then, I haven't heard my father's car drive up, but I could have missed it between slogging through my homework, trying to read the latest *Sports Illustrated*, and listening to the cassette recording of Anna's concert.

I don't want to wish him good night. The things I want to say to him, he doesn't want to hear. Why would I want him to have a good night? I hope he has a horrible night. I hope he can't sleep, and when he does, he has nightmares. Like maybe a nightmare in which he slaps me and I keel over dead. He gets arrested for murdering his own kid. Then a jury sends him to the electric chair. That would teach him. Or a nightmare in which he calls me a monster, and I really turn into one, some huge thing like Godzilla that picks him up in one paw and bites his head off.

"He still isn't home," Mom says.

She stares at the floor. I don't know what to say. What I think is: *Good! Now I don't have to see him until tomorrow morning.* But I can't say that. I can tell that she's bothered, and I don't want to make her feel worse.

"I haven't heard from him since a little after 8:00," she says. "He called to say he'd be late and not to wait for him." She makes a slight shrug. "I thought that meant for dinner, but maybe he meant staying up."

"Call him," I say.

She shakes her head. "He doesn't like it when I call. He says personal phone calls at the office should only be in cases of emergency, or a single one if he's going to be late. It doesn't look good if he frowns on everyone else's phone calls, and then gets one himself, even if it's so late only one person is left in the office to see it."

"He frowns on everything," I say, blurting it out before realizing that saying so, even if it's the truth, isn't being helpful.

A troubled look comes over Mom's face.

*Me and my big mouth.*

"I'm sorry," I say. "I shouldn't have said that."

She gives a sad shrug. "It's okay. I can't say that I disagree."

Silence hangs in the air. Mom looks like she's about to say something, but then reconsiders.

I make a wild guess, and try to help. "Don't worry. He'll be home."

She nods absently, then startled, looks at me sharply. "How do you do that?"

"Do what?"

"Don't play dumb with me. We've been through this before. It's like you can read my mind sometimes. It's spooky."

I shrug. "You looked worried. What else would you be worried about? The Russians? The Red Sox pitching staff? Are the Celtics too old to win the title this year? I thought you might be worried if he was coming home at all. It was just a guess."

"If you ever go into law enforcement," Mom says, shaking her head, "criminals won't stand a chance."

We both smile, but it's frozen and awkward. Then we fall silent for what feels like a long time.

It occurs to me yet again that if I were a different person, if I were a bit more respectful and kept my big mouth shut more often, we wouldn't be having this problem. A wave of guilt washes over me.

"I'm sorry," I say. "It's my fault you're worried. If I weren't—"

"No, no, no," she says, shaking her head. "Stop right there! This isn't about you. It's about him."

"But—"

"No buts from you, young man!"

I think I deserve a bit of the blame, in fact I *know* I deserve a bit of it. But I'll let her win this argument. It *is* mostly his fault. Nobody forced him to whack me. I zip my lip and just nod.

After a time, she says, "He's not a bad man."

There's nothing I can say to that. He's not bad like Jack the Ripper or Hitler or Al Capone. My father isn't evil. But he's awful compared to how he was just a little more than half a year ago.

"He's a good provider," she says. "He doesn't spend his time in bars, getting drunk and chasing women. He works hard."

Again, there's nothing I can say. I don't really care how much of a provider he is. I wish he stopped trying to be such a good provider, stop chasing after that next promotion. And stopped being such a jerk.

"He really isn't a bad man," she says again, and I begin to wonder if she's talking to herself as much as to me, trying to convince herself of what she's saying. Because she really isn't so sure. She says, "He didn't hit you because he liked it. He's honestly concerned about you. He doesn't want you to turn into something bad because we've 'spared the rod,' as he likes to say."

"So he's willing to turn into something bad himself?" I say, and instantly regret it. Once again, something slips out of my mouth before I get a chance to filter it.

"It isn't that easy," Mom says with a sigh. "There are people who feel the permissiveness of the hippies and the anti-war movement and all the protests these days are because we've got a generation of spoiled brats who weren't disciplined the way previous generations were. Kind of like that newspaper columnist said about you and the other boys during the basketball protests. Of course, I disagree completely.

"But when your father and I grew up, it was *expected* that a parent would administer as many spankings and the strap—a belt across the bare behind—and yes, as many slaps across the face as was needed to keep a child on the straight and narrow. I don't agree with it, and I won't tolerate any more of it, but you're hardly the only kid who hears harsh words from his father and gets a slap across the face. I can guarantee you that your father got slapped across the face by his father a *lot* more than you have. A *lot* more."

"Well, that makes me feel better," I say. I smile because in an odd way that maybe isn't really that odd at all, it *does* make me feel better thinking of my father getting slapped when he was my age. And when I think of him getting slapped a lot, my smile broadens.

Happy days are here again.

Mom blinks, her speech stopped dead in its tracks. Then she snorts with laughter, and shakes her head. Coming to give me a hug, she asks, "What am I going to do with you?"

I reply the same way I always do.

"I guess you're going to have to love me."

*

Those good feelings hit the brick wall the next morning. Mom has made French toast, my favorite, and I stack three slices on my plate, spread just a little butter on each, and top it with syrup. It smells great and tastes even better, the maple syrup sweet and each buttered slice making me want to cram another one in.

The brick wall is, of course, my father.

He comes down the stairs, wearing his usual dark suit, starched white shirt, and nondescript tie, carrying his tan briefcase. I have no idea when he came home—it was after I was asleep—but at least he came home. That's certainly what Mom wanted, and I suppose based on her feelings, I wanted it, too.

Although if it were just up to me, he could stay at work all day and night. I wouldn't miss him. He's already walked out of my life even though he's here right now.

Good riddance to bad rubbish.

I feel just the least bit guilty for thinking that phrase of Mom's, but that guilt flies right out the window when Dear Old

Dad walks robotically right past us and out the door as if we aren't even there, even though Mom calls out, "Andre, at least have some coffee!"

He doesn't even slow down. Not a glance at either one of us. Just a stone-faced look ahead.

Mr. Personality.

*

Out on the baseball field that afternoon, as a brisk wind gusts and the low-hanging clouds threaten to dump buckets of rain on us but don't, I continue to make my case for not being relegated to the freshmen team. I rip one line drive after another during batting practice. While others are batting, I flawlessly field the various infield positions, mostly shortstop and second base, except for one bad hop when a hard grounder hits a rock and bounces up high, almost giving me a second black eye but instead just skimming past my ear.

I even make three diving stops of hard-hit two-hoppers, bouncing back up to throw to first, almost certain to catch all but the fleetest of runners if the player taking batting practice had actually run to first. Those are just about as much fun as I can have on the baseball field. With each dive, my gray sweatshirt and sweat pants become more smeared with grass stains and clotted brown smudges of dirt. I feel the grit of the dirt on my face and beneath my fingernails.

A perfect measure of how much fun I'm having on the baseball field is how dirty my uniform or practice clothes or face get. By every measure, I'm having a ton of fun.

And I'm keeping my mouth shut. Even when as I'm batting, Moose asks from behind plate, "Is that a black eye you got there? What happened, your girlfriend beat you up?"

I ignore him. He's a moron, and I really don't care what he thinks anymore. Let him yap his way into the coach's doghouse. Not me.

Although I'm almost certainly still in Coach Kowalski's doghouse. Each day, I've raced to be one of the first guys out onto the field. Yesterday, he was standing alone by the twenty-foot-high metal backstop, a thick chaw of tobacco in his cheek, looking at his clipboard. So I called out, "Good afternoon, Coach," then trotted out to the crabgrass-infested, Little-League-sized freshman field. Today, all four of the coaches were clustered together, but they weren't talking so I just pounded my glove, and called out, "Great day for baseball!"

Coach Kowalski never indicates he's even noticed me. I'm as insignificant as a bug. Not even worth an editorial spit of tobacco juice.

I fear I'm buried so deep in his doghouse, I'll never get out.

*

A day later, on Friday, Coach Kowalski confirms my worst fears. Not with any spoken word, but with the team lists posted in the locker room after practice. The lists are taped onto the varnished white pine swinging doors that separate the locker room from the basketball courts. Everyone is crowded around them in a semicircle, at least ten deep, the rows of gray metal lockers behind us.

I'm in back because I was one of the last ones off the field, and the freshmen field is the farthest from the locker room. Since I'm short, the shortest of anyone trying out, I can't see a thing. Up front, others whoop for joy, groan, or curse.

I just wait. Player after player shoulders through the crowd from the front and emerges either with a smile or a dejected look on his face. Or in the case of some seniors whose positions were already known, an air of confidence.

Charlie Watkins emerges, looking conflicted. He sees me, and with a shake of his head and a grimace says, "It ain't fair, man."

I feel like I've been punched in the gut. I can't believe this has happened to him again. In basketball, he got stuck on the freshmen team and left there to rot because of Coach Abrams' bigotry. It took Abrams' firing to move Charlie to the JVs for a few games, and then a starting position on the varsity. It boggles my mind that the fiasco on the basketball team is being replayed. He and I are comparable baseball players. He's got more power. I'm better in the field.

Neither one of us belongs on the freshmen team. And he was smart enough to keep quiet while I yapped my way into Kowalski's doghouse.

"Again?" I ask. "I don't believe it."

He looks confused for a second, then winces. "No, Rabbit. I made JVs. So did Jessie." Jessie Stackhouse isn't great defensively at first base, but he'll hit a ton of homers. It would have been even more ridiculous to stick him on the freshmen team.

It takes a split second for me to get the message. My heart sinks.

"I didn't make it?" I ask, knowing the answer.

Charlie shakes his head. "It's a joke, man. And all because you spoke up that first day."

Coach Kowalski's words come back to me. *In that case, Labelle, enjoy your stay on the freshmen team. You can make your speeches to Coach Gilhooly.*

Me and my big mouth.

I nod woodenly. My gut clenches like a fist. I swallow hard. "Thanks, man." With my head swimming, I add, "Good luck on the JVs. Bet you make varsity soon."

I force a weak grin. I feel happy for Charlie, especially after all we went through during the basketball season. I'm happy for Jessie, too, even though he wasn't part of that, instead starring on the hockey team. But I can't help feeling sick over my own plight.

I wait until the crowd in front of the list thins out and I can see the result for myself. Charlie, Jessie, and one other freshman, CJ Powell, made the JVs. Halfway to the Promised Land of the varsity.

But not me. The troublemaker. The rebel. The spoiled brat with no respect for authority. The kid who can't keep his big mouth shut.

The monster.

*

Mom doesn't even have to ask when she picks me up after practice. She can tell just by the way I trudge to the car and throw my bag in the back seat with an extra oomph. Or if that isn't how she figures it out, I'm sure it's written all over my face.

"Oh, Rabbit," she says. She doesn't even hand me my snack. She just looks at me with sadness in her eyes.

"Let's go," I say. Mom nods, hands me my sandwich, and silently pulls away from the curb.

She seems to know that I can't even talk about it. So we sit there in silence with only the noise of the car humming along on the road in the background.

I don't touch the sandwich. I don't even peek to see what it is.

Finally, just before Wyoma Square, she turns on the radio. I guess the silence has become too awkward and she needs something to fill it. The station crackles at first, but then becomes a bit more clear with talk about the recent Presidential primary results up in New Hampshire.

"LBJ might not even get the Democratic nomination," Mom says, referring to President Lyndon Baines Johnson in her attempt at small talk. "That's almost inconceivable for a sitting president. McCarthy almost beat him on Tuesday in New Hampshire, and now talk is heating up that Bobby Kennedy will enter the race. The war is killing LBJ."

I couldn't possibly care less right now about Bobby Kennedy and all the other politicians. I don't even care about the war even though lots of boys only a few years older than I am are coming back from Vietnam in coffins, and the way things are going, there's no end in sight. In a couple of years, the Vietnam War might be the *only* thing I care about. But right now, I can't muster any concern at all.

There's not much I do care about right now.

"Do you think the Celtics will win it this year?" she asks, clicking off the radio, taking a different strategy to fill the silence.

I give her a look. I don't even care about the Celtics. Yesterday, I would have been blabbing about how, despite their age, they still have Bill Russell, and he hardly ever loses when it matters. Nine NBA championships and counting.

Today, though, I don't care.

"I'm sorry, honey," Mom says. Then she tries to find a silver lining in the cloud. "Maybe it was just because you're a freshman. The coaches need to see you play a few games. Then they'll realize their mistake."

Nice try, Mom.

"Charlie made JVs," I say with what feels like a Louisville Slugger down my throat. "So did Jessie. So did CJ Powell. All freshmen."

Mom's lips mouth the word "Oh" but she doesn't actually say it.

"None of them opened their big mouth," I say.

# CHAPTER 6

Aweek and a half later, the baseball teams are all playing their first games. I'm still stuck in Coach Kowalski's doghouse. The varsity is playing at Fraser Field, a stadium with more than 3,000 seats right next to Manning Bowl, where we played our football games. Both Fraser Field and Manning Bowl may be as run down as the city itself—some of the stands are rotted and blocked off, and graffiti covers some of the walls—but they represent the big time. The Rolling Stones played at Manning Bowl just two years ago. One of the Red Sox minor league teams played several seasons at Fraser Field a couple decades back.

Fraser Field is where we all want to get to. College scouts evaluating potential recruits, perhaps even scouts of major league teams. Grandstands. Outfield fences to hit home runs over instead of having to leg out inside-the-parkers. Concession stands. Cheerleaders. A few fans other than just family and girlfriends.

The big time.

The fields behind Lynn English is where the rest of us are now. They're the same fields the varsity and JVs practice on every day. The twenty-foot-high metal fence extends from the two backstops to divide the third-base foul area of the field on the right where the JVs play from the first-base foul area of the field on the left where we freshmen play. There's really no difference between the two fields.

But for me, there's all the difference in the world. Maybe like the Berlin Wall, separating the freedom and democracy of West Germany from East Germany's communist dictatorship.

On the other side of the fence from me is where Charlie, Jessie, CJ Powell, and the rest of the JVs are playing.

It's where I deserve to be.

The field on my side of that fence is every bit as first class as the JV's, and is a million times better than the Little-League-sized, crabgrass-festooned field the freshmen team practices on.

But I'm still on the wrong side of that fence.

My uniform is the same as theirs, gray with Lynn English stitched in script across the chest. We wear the same maroon stockings. My LEHS cap with the same two colors is the same as theirs.

But everything else is different.

I take my place at shortstop, looking longingly at that other field. Even as a bitter taste fills my mouth, I tell myself to stay focused or I'll never get my shot. I may never get a shot anyway thanks to my big mouth—thanks to Kowalski's unfairness—but I've got to give myself the best possible chance.

On the game's first pitch, I field a routine ground ball and fire to first in plenty of time to get the runner. Like a football player taking his first hit, that play locks my previously distracted mind onto the game where it belongs.

"Okay, let's go," I call out, and join in on the nonsense infield chatter of "No batter, no batter," and after our pitcher throws a strike, "You got him, you got him."

Two outs later, I trot in from the field, and grab a batting helmet and two bats. I'm leading off, and it's time to show what I've got. I swing the two bats a few times, then drop the extra one and match my swings to the opposing pitcher's warm-up throws. My focus wavers briefly when I hear the crack of the bat and whoops of joy from the other field—*where I ought to be*—but then I push all that away.

Nothing but me and the Everett pitcher. And he doesn't stand a chance.

He's squat, chunky, and powerful, so I've given him the nickname Mini-Tank. His dark brown hair pokes out from beneath a navy blue cap with the white letters SHS. From what I could see in warm-ups, he's got a good fastball that pops loud in the catcher's mitt.

But it ain't close to good enough.

"Play ball!" the stocky umpire, clad entirely in black, calls out.

I step into the batter's box, tap the far edge of the plate, and dig in. The infield starts its chatter. The catcher, squatting behind the plate wearing his mask, navy blue chest protector and shin guards, chirps away in an attempt to distract me.

"Nice black eye," he says, his voice muffled behind his mask. Without realizing it, he repeats Moose Mahoney's taunt. "Your girlfriend beat you up again?"

After the first two days, the black eye had become so noticeable—its gray, thin, curving line beneath the eye growing wider and turning purple—I stopped using makeup. There was no way to cover it up completely, so the makeup just made things worse. I told everyone the black eye came from a bad hop in the infield, tried to act as if I was proud of it, then changed the subject by complaining about the crabgrass-infested field we have to practice on. Most everyone accepted the lie.

Back home, I could sense Mom's blood pressure rise every time she looked at it. She'd purse her lips, and if my father wasn't around, shake her head. He, of course, acted as if it were invisible.

He acted as if *I* were invisible.

Not that I cared.

Slowly, the discoloration faded and it's mostly gone now. Hardly noticeable, but clearly still visible enough for the catcher to see. But I can't let myself get distracted. So I ignore him.

He switches to a different tactic.

"Hey midget, you're on the wrong field," he says. "The Little League field is down the street."

Somewhere deep inside I smile. Like I've never been called a midget before. I'll take that over references to my father hitting me any day. I tune the mouthy catcher out, just like turning the TV volume all the way down. As far as I'm concerned, he isn't even there.

It's just me and Mini-Tank, standing on the mound. And he has no chance.

I'm taking the first pitch no matter what. It's what Ted Williams almost always did, and if he wasn't the greatest hitter of all time, he sure was close. Taking that first pitch is what he recommends in his book, *The Science of Hitting*, a title I've I read and re-read so many times the binding has fallen apart. I almost have every page memorized.

But Mini-Tank gives me a break on the first pitch. I don't have to go down a strike just to time that good fastball of his because it's inside. A ball. Now I've got the timing down, *and* I'm ahead in the count.

"He's kinda wild," the catcher yaps. "He ain't trying to hit you, but he might. Could break a midget like you in half."

Just me and Mini-Tank. And he has no chance.

The next pitch is a good one, but nowhere near good enough. It's a hard fastball over the outside part of the plate. I step into it and drive a rocket into the gap between center and right field.

I'm off with the crack of the bat. I'm motoring around first base and see the ball bouncing between the two outfielders. As they chase after it, I fly around second and race into third where dark-haired Russell Blake, who's acting as our third base coach because he isn't in the lineup, has his hands raised, telling me to stop but not to bother sliding.

Standing on third, I turn and see their second baseman running onto the infield dirt, ready to throw home if I go for it. I take a step off the base, but make only a half-hearted fake to the plate, then retreat to third.

A stand-up triple. Not a bad start to the game. Not a bad start to the season, even if—

*Even if I'm stuck on the Freshmen team.*

But I block that out. Focus. Not a bad start to the season. I hear my teammates cheer, then I hear my mom yell out loud and clear, "Way to go, Rabbit!"

Mini-Tank, however, strikes out the next two batters. It looks like my triple may be wasted. So with the third baseman playing back, no longer needing to worry about a play at the plate, and with Mini-Tank no longer pitching out of the stretch so he can throw over and keep me close, I decide to take matters into my own hands.

As he begins his windup, I take off for home plate. I'm not actually trying to steal home. I'm going only far enough to catch Mini-Tank's eye, and with any luck induce a balk, an illegal interruption of his throwing motion.

Sure enough, as I race toward home and just before I slam on the brakes to race even faster back to third, Mini-Tank stops in mid-motion, then attempts to cover up his blunder by resuming the pitch.

But it's such a flagrant balk that the umpire moves out from behind the plate, waves his arms, and makes the call. He awards me home plate and the run. As Mini-Tank shakes his head in frustration, I trot home. I step on the plate and give the big-mouthed catcher a big smile.

By the time I get to the plate next time, Everett leads, 2–1. I wonder if Mini-Tank is going to drill me because of the balk, making me pay for embarrassing him, but if he wants to put me on base in a one-run game, I'll take it.

He does brush me back with the first pitch, but the second is a fastball on the inside of the plate. I rip it down the left field line and don't stop until I'm on second base. Mini-Tank throws twice to second base to keep me close or even pick me off, but in the process seems to lose his focus on the batter, Matt Gallucci. Matt, who's a slow but big offensive lineman on the football team, rips another double down the left field line, and I easily score to tie the game. Three batters later, we lead, 4–2, and we've knocked Mini-Tank out of the game.

In my final at bat, with us up 5–3, and Moose on first, I send another rocket into the gap between center and right. Moose lumbers around second and heads into third, apparently ready to stop there for oxygen even though the third base coach is waving him home, but Coach Gilhooly roars, "Move it, Moose! Move it!" and he keeps moving. I glide into third for another standup triple, and a sacrifice fly brings me home.

Matt pitches an uneventful seventh inning—high school games go seven innings, not nine—and we've got a satisfying win in our first game. A nice way to kick off the season. And with a double and two triples in three at bats, as well as flawless fielding at shortstop, I've made the best possible case for a promotion.

But with how Coach Kowalski feels about me, will it even matter?

*

Friday rolls around, and I'm still on the freshmen team, leading off and playing shortstop. This game, our second, is also at home, as is the JV's, so we're once again playing back-to-back on the fields behind the school.

I feel no closer to getting on the good side of that fence—the JV side—than I was three days ago. Coach Gilhooly complimented me after the first game, saying, "Heckuva game, Rabbit! Heckuva game!" but he doesn't make the decisions that really matter. Coach Kowalski does.

And Kowalski still hasn't spoken to me, or given any indication he knows I'm even alive. When he sees me coming out to the practice field, he continues whatever conversation he's having with the other three coaches, but turns his back to me. The most I get is a spit of his tobacco juice.

A double, two triples, and three runs scored in three at bats hasn't even gotten me to the door of the doghouse. I'm still buried deep inside. Might as well be six feet under. So I tell myself to claw my way to that door.

In the first inning, I hit a double into the left-center gap, steal third, and trot in on a sacrifice fly. Next time up, I hit a screaming line drive right at the third baseman. Couldn't hit it any harder. But it's right at the guy, a freckle-faced, squat redhead, and he nabs it for my first out of the year.

The next two times, though, I hit singles, then steal both second and third. But I'm stranded both times even with an unsuccessful attempt to induce a balk. We lose, 8–3, and though Coach Gilhooly congratulates me on my hitting and two diving stops in the field, he doesn't look me in the eye.

He knows I'm being treated unfairly. Probably knows it's going to continue.

I grab my glove and glumly head for the showers, but Charlie intercepts me behind the backstop. Although the JV game ended ten or fifteen minutes ago, he stuck around.

"How you doing, man?" he asks.

I shrug. "We lost."

"I know," he says, and we start walking to the rear entrance. "How *you* doing?"

"Rather be on your side of the fence."

"I hear ya. It ain't right."

I glumly nod. We move from the grass field onto the pavement. Our cleats click with every step. The smell of the asphalt fills our nostrils.

"Anybody got you out yet?" Charlie asks.

"Lined out to third base. Kid's glove is still smokin.'"

Charlie chuckles. "You stealing bases be like taking candy from babies."

"Yeah," I say. "A bit like you on the freshman basketball team."

"Just like it," he says. "That's what I wanted to talk to you about."

I look at him and raise an eyebrow.

"You remember what you told me?" Charlie asks.

"When?"

"When I got frustrated 'cause I was stuck on the freshmen team. It was too easy. Felt like I could score forty blindfolded."

"Blindfolded?"

"Blindfolded could have at least scored thirty."

I give a small laugh, but have no idea what he's getting at. "What did I tell you?"

"You told me to keep knocking at the door. Coach Abrams would have to let me in."

I remember that now. Yeah, that's pretty much what I told Charlie. It was all I could think of.

"Well," Charlie says, "shoe on the other foot now. Time you practice what you preach. You just gotta knock on that door. Knock that sucker down."

Charlie's right. I nod.

"Gonna put my fist through that door," I say. "It's going down."

*

When I get on the phone with Anna several hours later, she offers me her own encouragement and thoughtful advice. Not surprisingly, it doesn't involve any fists through doors.

"I probably shouldn't say this," she says. "It may come out all wrong."

"No, tell me!" I urge her, holding the phone tighter as I sit on the floor inside my father's otherwise empty home office. My back is against the closed door, the long, black phone cord snaked beneath the door to the phone on its stand just outside the room.

"Well…I never thought much about these kind of things until I met you," she says. "They seemed like adult things, serious things, and I wasn't ready for them. I thought, 'I'm just a kid,' and then, 'I'm just a teenager.' But you've made me think about them. You know?"

"I guess," I say hesitantly, not sure where she's going with this.

"Now you've taken a stand based on your principles, just like you did in the basketball protests," she says. "You're having to pay for it. It isn't fair, but think of those three Civil Rights workers in Mississippi who were killed simply because they were trying to organize black voters."

"Chaney, Schwerner, and Goodman," I say.

"Yes. And all those who died before them, buried in that Mississippi swamp," Anna says. "They *died* for their principles. Or think of those who have marched for Civil Rights and been beaten by police or had attack dogs sicced on them."

"What does that have to do with—"

"Think of Dr. King getting jailed because he led a nonviolent protest. A nonviolent protest protected by the Bill of Rights."

"Yes, but—"

"You might not want to hear this, and maybe I shouldn't say it, but sometimes there's just a price that has to be paid for taking a stand. It isn't fair, but life isn't always fair. I know that's the kind of things our parents always tell us—life isn't fair! life isn't fair!—and we get sick of hearing it, but it's true.

"Sometimes you have to pay a price you shouldn't have to pay, but that's just the way it is. You and the black basketball players had to pay a price. Jamaal got hurt so bad he missed almost the rest of the season. You lost some of your best friends."

I think of wise-cracking, freckle-faced Jeff Goodwin and Paul DiSimone, Paul so quiet he couldn't get a word in edgewise when Jeff was around. Best of friends of mine before the protests. Shared most of my classes with them. Friends no more. I don't miss them, because they showed their true colors, but yes…I still miss those friendships and the laughter.

"So now you have to pay a price on the baseball team," Anna says. "Maybe for just a few more games. Hopefully, that's all it is. But maybe it's for the whole season. And maybe it hurts a little more because you're so good at baseball, and you already sacrificed during the basketball season. So you're all sacrificed-out, if you know what I mean.

"I know this is easy for me to say. I'd hate it if it happened to me with the orchestras and bands I play in. I'd really hate it. But when you get feeling bad about it, just realize that you're doing the right thing. You can live with yourself, you can live with the sacrifice you made, because you did the right thing. You had the courage to stand up for what you believed in. And as much as it makes you mad, the price you're paying now is nothing compared to what so many others have had to pay."

Her words hit me over the head like a baseball bat. I've been such a baby about this. In Mom's words, I've been making a mountain out of a molehill.

"I'm not saying it's nothing!" Anna adds with an air of concern in her voice when I don't immediately reply. "I don't mean that. I know baseball is really important to you."

"No, you're right," I say. "You're absolutely right. Next time I get feeling bad for myself, I need to think of Chaney, Schwerner, and Goodman. Malcolm X and Dr. King and all the others."

"Yes!" Anna says with an almost gasp of relief. "I was afraid that came out all wrong."

"No, it came out all right," I say. "Absolutely right."

It wasn't what I'd wanted to hear. But it was what I needed to hear.

*

Our third game comes the next Tuesday, and still nothing has changed. Neither Coach Kowalski nor Coach Gilhooly has said a word to me about my performances and the JVs. They're giving me the same silent treatment as Dear Old Dad, although Coach Gilhooly at least seems uncomfortable about it. I'm sure he's just taking orders.

Still, it seems like the worst possible hat trick ever—to use one of Jessie Stackhouse's hockey terms—to have three of the most important men in my life unwilling to speak to me.

But I'm taking Charlie's and Anna's advice to heart. I'm going to keep beating on the door until Kowalski has to open it, and I'm not going to feel sorry for myself. If this is the price I have to pay, I'll hold my head high like Dr. King and try to make the coaches ashamed for how they're treating me.

This game is on the road, at Marblehead. It's a town that has given birth to one of Mom's newest pet phrases. When the truth belatedly dawns on someone, she says, "Light finally dawns on marble head." She says it occasionally about me, but I bet she thinks it even more often about my father's marble head. In his case, though, I think the term Red Sox manager Dick Williams uses for first baseman George "Boomer" Scott, who strikes out a lot, is even better: cement head.

In any case, we take the bus to the Marblehead field, I keep my mouth shut, and I try to beat that door down. Try to bust it to splinters.

We win 8–5. I get three doubles and score three runs. The only time Marblehead gets me out is when its center fielder makes a spectacular diving catch in the right-center alley. If the ball got by him, I'd have gotten an inside-the-park home run for sure. But he nabbed it, leaving me standing there with my mouth open, wondering what this guy is doing on the freshmen team.

I can only guess that he's got a big mouth, too.

*

Finally on Thursday after practice, I approach Coach Gilhooly. Everyone else has headed inside, even Tony, the equipment manager, with the two gray duffle bags containing the balls, bats, and helmets slung over both shoulders. So Coach and I are alone on the freshman practice field. He's wearing his usual warm-up suit and cap, and is scribbling notes on his clipboard. My own practice clothes, my gray jersey and sweatpants, are covered with grass stains. Dirt is caked beneath my fingernails. I've dived after enough ground balls to be pretty sure my face is caked with mud and dirt, too.

"Coach, can I talk to you?"

He glances up and sees we're alone. He looks around with the nervous, uncomfortable appearance of a student who's just gotten hit with a pop quiz he isn't prepared for. Or one who's gotten caught cheating.

"Of course," he says, even though everything about him screams that he'd rather be anywhere else on Earth than here.

I decide to get right to the point. I won't be disrespectful or do anything that will push me even deeper into the doghouse, but I've got to know.

"Do you think I deserve to be on the JV team?"

Coach Gilhooly's eyes tighten, as if he's in pain. He looks toward the varsity practice field, then back to me. But his eyes don't meet mine. He looks up in the clouds.

"That's a complicated question," he finally answers.

I don't see how it's complicated at all. It's really pretty easy. But I can't say that.

"What else do I have to do, Coach? Whatever it is, I'll do it."

That pained look in his eyes tightens even further. He looks again to the varsity field, as if Coach Kowalski can somehow bail him out. Or if maybe Kowalski can do his own dirty work instead of dumping it on Coach Gilhooly.

"It isn't that easy," he says. "Sorry, Rabbit. I've got to run."

And he brushes past me as if I'm not even there.

# CHAPTER 7

Everything changes that night.

I'm upstairs in my bedroom working on an essay for English class, waiting for Dear Old Dad to get home so we can eat dinner or for Mom to give up on him and we eat alone, when I hear a strange sort of shriek downstairs.

My mother. I've never heard that sound from her before.

Ever.

I race downstairs and find her in the front room watching Walter Cronkite on the CBS News. Her eyes are wide, her face pale, and a hand covers her mouth.

"What—"

But that's as far as I get before her hand shoots out in a stopping gesture, silencing me.

I lock onto the black-and-white image of Cronkite on the TV, somberly talking about a shooting. I hear "Memphis" and "fleeing white man" and then "apostle of non-violence."

And as I put the pieces of the puzzle together, Cronkite provides the missing name.

*Dr. Martin Luther King.* He's been shot.

*No!* An awful taste forms in the back of my throat. A sick feeling fills my gut. *No!*

How could this happen to a man—a great man!—whose message is one of peace? Who had returned to Memphis to prove he could control the anger—the justified anger—of those who marched with him. Who was even awarded a Nobel Peace Prize a couple years ago for his efforts to achieve Civil Rights without violence.

In a just world, Dr. King should be the *last* person shot.

But this isn't a just world.

"Will he be okay?" I ask when Cronkite fades to a commercial.

"I don't know," Mom says, then adds, "They don't know. Not yet. Or they aren't saying."

We stare at each other, and shake our heads.

*

There's no way I can concentrate on my essay for English class now. It isn't due until Monday, but I had hoped to get a head start on it. Now, though, who cares? Certainly not me.

My eyes stay glued to the TV even as it returns to normal programming. With Mom's approval, I switch from Channel 7 to 5 and to 4. They're all the same, broadcasting stuff that doesn't matter at all. How can anyone care about *Daniel Boone*, *Cimarron Strip*, or *The Flying Nun* at a time like this? Even Channel 2, the public broadcasting station, is showing its usual programming.

I try the UHF channels, 38 and 56, with their snowy images improved only marginally by me holding the circular middle part of the antenna, its two outer metal rods shooting up and out from the TV top in a V shape. Nothing there either, although I hardly expected it.

So I switch back to Channel 7 and wait for Walter Cronkite to return.

The phone rings, and Mom rushes to answer it. She talks in hushed tones, then pokes her head around the corner.

"That was your father," she says. "He says we're to lock the doors and stay inside. He's on his way home. He expects rioting and violence, especially if Dr. King dies, but he hopes he can get home before it starts. And maybe it'll just be Boston and the really big cities. If it's here in Lynn…" She draws in a deep breath and shakes her head. "You know your father. You know how he thinks. He says we might finally be grateful he paid so much attention to buying a house in a part of the city that's almost one-hundred-percent white. According to him, the blacks will probably just burn down their own neighborhoods."

*

I hold my breath that the nightmare doesn't come true. That Dr. King will recover, and will continue to be the voice of equality and non-violence. That his voice will continue to ring out, and not be silenced by the forces of evil.

But the nightmare comes true.

With our doors locked and Mom and I sitting on the edge of our seats on the sofa, Walter Cronkite appears on the TV screen. He's wearing his dark-rimmed glasses. His face is drawn and somber. Mom takes hold of my hand and grips it tightly.

"Dr. Martin Luther King, the apostle of non-violence in the civil rights movement, has been shot to death in Memphis, Tennessee," Cronkite says. Mom gasps. She tightens her grip on my hand so hard it hurts, while the other hand flies up to cover her mouth. I feel like I've been punched in the gut. Cronkite continues, "Police have issued an all-points bulletin for a well-dressed, young white man seen running from the scene. Officers also reportedly chased and fired on a radio-equipped car containing two white men.

"Dr. King was standing on the balcony of a second-floor hotel room tonight when, according to a companion, a shot was fired from across the street. In the friend's words, the bullet exploded in his face."

Cronkite goes on to describe Dr. King as "the Nobel Peace Prize winner," which is surely the saddest and most sickening of ironies. Cronkite reports that sporadic violence has already erupted in the black sections of Memphis, and people are spilling out, dazed, into the streets of Harlem. A clip is shown of President Johnson making a plea for peace, and then a clip of Dr. King speaking just last night of how cities like Memphis have attempted to deny the First Amendment privileges of freedom of assembly and freedom of speech.

Cronkite is on for only four or five minutes, but it feels like forever and at the same time, only an instant.

The forces of evil had attempted to silence Dr. King's voice by trying to deny him and his followers the right to march peacefully for Civil Rights, but they hadn't succeeded.

Now they've silenced Dr. King forever.

*

I'm supposed to call Anna just once each night and then only talk for five minutes to keep the phone bill down. But even though we've already talked, I need to call her again. Not because I'm worried that she's in danger because of any possible riots. She lives in a section of the city that is every bit as white as the one I live in.

I just need to talk to her.

But even though I've never called him once on the phone, and don't even know his phone number, I need to talk to Charlie even more. It's not like he's my only black friend. There's Jamaal and Jessie, as well as all the black members of basketball team who were also involved in the protest, and my classmate Mike Thompson. I consider them all friends, and perhaps I should try to call them all even if my father goes through the roof when he gets the phone bill.

But none of my other black friends have been through the experience Charlie and I shared of having Hells Angels attack our car while we were stopped at a red light. They tried to kick in the windows while yelling the worst of racial epithets, then one of them pointed a gun at me. I stared at the barrel of that revolver, sure I was going to die. An experience like that forges a special bond.

So I look up his number in the phone book and call. His mother answers on the fourth ring with a shaking voice that makes me sure she's been crying. I wonder for a moment if I've made a mistake in calling. Perhaps I'm intruding on a sacred moment, like a stranger's car cutting in on a funeral procession. I'm just a stupid white kid, barging in where I don't belong. But if I've made a mistake, it's too late now. I certainly can't hang up.

"Hello, Mrs. Watkins," I say. "This is Rabbit." When she doesn't respond, I add, "Charlie's friend." And then my brain finally kicks in, and I belatedly say, "I am so, so sorry about the news."

She chokes out the words, "I'll get Charlie," and then sets the receiver down.

It feels like forever before he picks up the phone.

"Hey, man," I say. "I just had to call and say how sorry I am. This is such awful, awful news."

"Yeaaah," Charlie says, stretching the word out, low and mournful. As if something deep inside him has died.

And I wonder if something inside a lot of us, not just black people, has died. My throat tightens. I can't swallow. I don't really know what else to say. I should have thought this out before making the phone call.

But thinking first isn't one of my strong suits.

I finally manage to say, "I can't believe this has happened."

His response cuts me open like a sharp knife.

He says, "I can."

# CHAPTER 8

The next day, my father doesn't want me to go to school. We're eating breakfast, but not at the dining room table like Mom usually insists. Instead, my father and I are seated on opposite ends of the front room sofa, our bowls of oatmeal on TV trays in front of us, while Mom stands at the front room entrance. All our eyes are glued to the RCA black-and-white TV on the far side of the room, and the latest news it's broadcasting about Dr. King's shooting.

About Dr. King's *murder*.

The FBI and local police are looking for a white male driving a white Mustang, but they haven't found him yet. Last night, the Memphis mayor, a white man who'd been trying to stop Dr. King from marching, invoked a curfew, but violence still erupted, including sniper fire at police. Fires have been set in Chicago. Looters are taking out their anger and frustration in Washington, DC.

The newscast repeats the clips from last night of President Johnson calling for peace and Dr. King speaking of the freedom of speech and the freedom of assembly. A new clip plays of Bobby Kennedy breaking the news of Dr. King's death to a largely black audience. They cry out in agony. Kennedy also calls for peace, and speaks of his own brother, the late President John F. Kennedy, being shot and killed by a gunman.

I watch as if I'm in a trance, letting my oatmeal grow cold until Mom reminds me to eat. Even then, I eat robotically, not realizing there are slices of banana in the oatmeal until what's probably my fourth or fifth bite.

I feel dead inside. My gut clenches and unclenches. It's at the same time hollow and yet also filled with a heavy, leaden sadness.

And if this is how I feel, I can't even imagine how Charlie, Jamaal, Jessie, and all my other black friends feel. There must be a total sense of hopeless desperation on the other side of that racial wall.

None of us says a word until the news gives way to a commercial.

"Rabbit, you stay home from school today," my father says, even though he's dressed for work in his usual black suit, white shirt, and dark tie. He eyes the door, clearly itching to bolt for it. But he gives me a hard look. "There are Negroes at your school—not a lot but enough—and there's no telling what they'll do. My secretary will be monitoring the news, and I'll come flying home if there are problems. The violence is going to spread, mark my words. The big cities are going to explode. It'll make last summer's riots look like a picnic."

Although I wasn't aware of those riots at the time up in rural Maine—if it didn't have to do with sports back then, I wasn't paying attention—I've since learned about how they erupted in big cities like Detroit, Newark, and Milwaukee.

"This is the worst possible thing that could have happened for people like us," my father says.

My jaw drops. I must not have heard him correctly.

"For people like us?" I ask, incredulous. "The worst possible thing for *white people?*" When my father just nods absently, I say, "I thought you hated Dr. King."

"I did," he says distractedly. "But—"

He stops and shakes his head as if to clear the cobwebs. "I didn't actually *hate* the man. That's too strong a word. I didn't approve of what he was doing, making every last angry Negro even more angry. That's why all our big cities have been such powder kegs, waiting to explode."

I want to jump in and challenge this point. It seems foolish beyond belief, perhaps deliberately so. I have to all but literally bite my tongue to stay silent.

"But at least King was better than the Black Power crowd," my father says. "King believed in non-violence, even if he couldn't always control his people. But some of those others…" He shakes his head again. "This could get very, very dangerous."

He stands up, takes three strides to the front door, and grabs his tan briefcase, propped against the wall. He turns back to face me. He glances at my mother, then back to me.

"Fortunately, we might not have enough blacks here in Lynn for it to be dangerous," he says. "And if they decide to burn down their own neighborhoods, it'll be miles away from us."

I feel my eyes widen at this casual dismissal of lives other than our own, as if they don't matter at all, even though this isn't the first time I've heard him mouth these words.

"I don't want you taking any chances," he says to me. "There are plenty of Negroes in that school, and who knows what state of mind they'll be in. They might attack the first white face they see. It won't be safe, so I want you to stay home. Since it's Friday, it'll only cost the one day, and I'm guessing not a lot of teaching will get done today anyway. Stay home, and we'll see how things stand on Monday."

He turns to leave, but my words stop him dead in his tracks.

"I'm going," I say.

The words are out of my mouth before I realize it. Perhaps they were inevitably coming out as soon as he dismissed the burning down of black neighborhoods as being of no concern because they were miles away.

*Because they don't matter.*

Or maybe I'm fooling myself. Maybe I'm just a rotten kid who likes to cause trouble. That's certainly what my father thinks, and so does Coach Kowalski.

Either way, the words are out.

Blood drains from my father's face. "What did you say?"

"I said I'm going." As if there really was any question about what I said. My father heard me the first time loud and clear.

"Rabbit," Mom says, trying to intercede. "Maybe you should listen—"

"*He never listens!*" my father bellows. He strides back to me, and for a brief moment I'm sure he's going to backhand me across the face again and give me another black eye. Instead, he bends down, and puts his suddenly flushed face inches away from mine. I can smell his minty aftershave and the slight smell of oatmeal on his breath. But mostly I see his wide eyes burning with fury, their black pupils forcing me to stare only at them.

I crazily think of that childhood story, *Rikki-Tikki-Tavi,* and how in it, the hero mongoose must avoid being mesmerized by the cobras' deadly eyes. I feel like that now, unable to turn away from my father's furious glare.

"You may think the Negroes you know are your friends, but they aren't," my father says through gritted teeth. "They aren't like us." He steps back. "You want to go get yourself killed by those animals? Go ahead! See if I care."

Mom shrieks. "Andre, you don't mean that!"

He strides for the front door, but she throws herself at him, wrapping her arms around him. "*You don't mean that! Say you don't mean that!*" She begins to cry. "I won't let you leave this house until you take that back."

But my father breaks loose of her grasp, and pushes her away. Not hard, but she's off balance so she stumbles, almost falling to the floor before righting herself against the wall.

I shoot to my feet, fists clenched, ready to charge. But he makes no move at my mother, and she warily keeps her distance, leaning against the wall as if needing it for support.

"I meant every last word!" he says, then leaves, slamming the door behind him.

Mom looks at me, horrified. I stare back at her.

*You want to go get yourself killed by those animals? Go ahead! See if I care.*

Seconds later, he's back. An embarrassed look covers his face as he ducks back inside the door. He shifts awkwardly on his feet.

"I didn't really mean that," he says. "Of course I didn't. Of course I care. I was just angry. But Rabbit, you get me furious with your insolence. I don't know what to do with you sometimes."

He stares at me, then Mom, then me again.

And then he leaves.

I suppose it's good that he came back and said what he said. Better than if he hadn't, and left his raw hatred for me unedited. But I wonder if somewhere in the ugliest part of his brain, a part he can't even acknowledge, he really meant every last word.

*

Mom is all teary-eyed when she drives me to school. I'll admit, I'm a basket case, too. My father's words keep rattling around in my head. He tried to take them back, but once some things get said, they can never get un-said.

*You want to go get yourself killed by those animals? Go ahead! See if I care.*

He's right that I can be a rotten kid sometimes, and I make lots of my own troubles. I get that. I know I need to keep my big mouth shut more often. And just because he says awful things about black people, including a great friend like Charlie, that doesn't automatically make *everything* my father says wrong. I don't have to instinctively feel the need to defy him *all* the time. And I sup-pose I should remember that until he got angry—until I made him angry—his thoughts were to protect me.

But my brain still bounces back and forth, like a ball at a tennis match, between him calling my friends animals and then saying, "See if I care." The volley goes back and forth for a while—degrade my friends with the worst of insults…profess not to care at all about me…degrade my friends…discard me like a piece of trash.

Eventually there's a winner. Maybe it means I'm just a selfish jerk, but my brain latches on to what hurts me most. Those four words.

*See if I care.*

No matter how often my father and I argue, and no matter how often I feel total disgust and sometimes actual hatred toward him, I still feel crushed by those words. It's hard to believe in six months we've gone from happily playing catch in the backyard and discussing the Boston sports teams to this.

I suppose today is a day for feeling crushed in multiple ways.

"Are you sure you don't want to stay home?" Mom asks, as we near the school. Even though she shares none of my father's bigotry, especially after that day last fall when I convinced her to give Charlie a ride home and she could see past his intimidating Afro to the great person he is, she's still a mom. Protective. A worrier.

And my father's words scare her. That, and the news reports of the violence breaking out across the country. It took a lot to convince her I'd be fine and that I wasn't going just to spite my father, responding in a reflex reaction to him saying I couldn't. As soon as we pulled out of the driveway, she locked her car door and told me to lock mine, too. When I asked her why, she snapped, "Just do it." Ever since, she's been glancing around nervously.

I know she'd be happy if I told to her take me back home, but I can't do it. And not just because I'm a rotten kid intent on defying my jerk of a father. I want to see Charlie and my other black friends.

I *need* to see them.

I need to let them know face-to-face how saddened I am at their loss—at *our* loss. I also want to see Anna—that's true every day—but today that's secondary.

This is not a day for playing hooky.

*

Charlie isn't at his locker. Neither are Jamaal or Jessie. They might still be here today, just not at their lockers. I just don't know. I've never stopped by their lockers before school before. Maybe they chose to stay home. Disappointed, I head to Anna's locker, my usual destination before school starts, but she isn't there either.

Isn't anyone here today?

I spot Janice Downing, a black classmate with whom I share several classes, heading in the opposite direction alone, holding two textbooks to her chest. She's wearing a navy blue dress with white trim. Pretty, with a modest Afro, she's just about the shyest person I've ever met. She never speaks in class unless called on.

"Janice," I say, startling her. She steps back with a soft intake of breath, then sees it's me. Her bloodshot eyes widen ever so slightly. We stand in the middle of the corridor. She blinks. Other students stream around us in both directions.

"I'm sorry for what happened last night," I say. "For Dr. King's death. It's a great loss. A loss for us all. But especially for you." I inwardly wince. That didn't sound right. I fumble for the right words. "Especially for black people. But for all people who believe in equality and justice."

Tears pool in her eyes. She visibly gulps, nods, then looks down at the floor.

I suddenly feel foolish, my words inept and clumsy. Maybe even patronizing. What words can possibly capture what has happened? What should I have said? Should I have said anything at all?

I stand there awkwardly as more students move past us.

"Well…" I say, and then don't know what else to add. I certainly can't say "Have a nice day" or any of the other usual ways to end a conversation. Finally, I manage, "I gotta go." She nods and we move on.

In homeroom, I see about one out of every three or four seats is empty. Over the crackling, static-filled PA system, the principal, Mr. Saunders, announces that first period is cancelled. We are all to head immediately to the auditorium for an assembly.

Inside the auditorium, our homeroom class is directed down the left aisle toward the front. Between the two aisles, there are rows of twenty middle seats, with ten seats off to the left and another ten to the right. We're herded into two left rows halfway to the elevated podium where the principal, vice principal, and one other man I don't recognize—all wearing dark suits, white shirts, and dark ties—are seated to the right of a lectern. The buzz of conversation fills the air, but there are none of the usual outbursts of laughter. It's a somber buzz.

Opposite us in a far right row off the other aisle, Charlie stands stone-faced, his jaw set. He sees me just before he sits down and gives a grim nod. Next to him, Jamaal, his anger visible for anyone to see, glares at me for a few long seconds—as if I shot Dr. King myself—then looks away.

I keep looking back at Jamaal for some explanation or at least a nod of recognition that we are on the same side, but get none. And I suppose I can't blame him. He came to Lynn just last summer from down South where the lines between black and white aren't subtle at all. They're impenetrable walls that seem miles high. Until Charlie convinced him otherwise, Jamaal had no intention of having a white friend. I might be a teammate, but not a friend. And I can guess that Dr. King's death—his murder—has erected those walls yet again between Jamaal and me.

To be honest, I can't blame him. After what has happened, I can understand the distrust. I can only hope that it's temporary and that it hasn't bled into hatred, and that the trust and friendship that has been lost can eventually be won back.

When all the classes have filed in, Mr. Saunders steps to the lectern and adjusts the microphone. He asks that we all stand and observe a moment of silence.

It seems to last forever.

Finally, he breaks the silence. He introduces the mayor, Mr. Sullivan, a short, squat, balding man of about fifty, who says all the right things, but doesn't say anything at all. He gives tribute to Dr. King for being an inspiration to everyone, especially young people, and for representing the highest of ideals.

Of course, all of that is true, but it's the safe kind of thing that politicians have to say to avoid controversy, to avoid offending people like my father and apparently Anna's father. No one can argue that Dr. King was an inspiration.

But why not speak up about the injustices that forced him to march? Why not speak up about how black people are denied the right to vote in so many states down South? How they are paid so much less than their white counterparts? How a mean-spirited bigot like George Wallace, whose greatest achievement in life has been attempting to stop a black student from entering his lily-white University of Alabama, is now a serious candidate for the President of the United States?

How about the problems we have up here in supposedly liberal Massachusetts? How people can cheer Celtics star Bill Russell when he's on the basketball court, but try to prevent him from buying a home in their suburban neighborhood? And when he buys a home anyway, someone breaks in and trashes his house, including spreading racial epithets on his walls and actually going to the bathroom—and I'm not talking urination—on his bed.

How about just a few months ago this very school having a racist basketball coach who used the N-word to describe the way Charlie and Jamaal played? How about the gang of thugs who assaulted those of us who protested those actions, wielding baseball bats and breaking bones, attempting to break our spirits?

Why can't our mayor say something *honest* instead of these empty platitudes? Why is Dr. King's legacy of non-violence the only thing of substance the mayor comments on? Does the mayor really think that Dr. King's successors will be able to indefinitely hold off the violence and cap the righteous rage of black people?

The mayor finishes his speech, folds his papers of notes and tucks them in the inside pocket of his suit. After polite applause, he rushes off to the next school where he'll no doubt repeat his worthless babble.

*

I almost forget there's a baseball game to play today.

It seems so pointless. I wonder what the professional sports are doing. President Johnson has called for a national day of mourning on Sunday, but can today's grief be postponed? Isn't it at its absolute worst today?

Why are we playing?

But we do.

The freshmen team wins, 7–3. The JVs, playing without Jessie Stackhouse, who didn't come to school today, lose, 5–4, despite a three-run home run by Charlie.

But who cares?

# CHAPTER 9

After the game, Mom and I are barely inside the front door when my father arrives. He looks nervous as he locks the door, sets down his briefcase beside it, and pushes his black-framed glasses to the bridge of his nose. For a brief, foolish moment I wonder if he's going to make a sheepish apology for the raw hatred for me he displayed this morning. Something more than, *I didn't mean that, you just made me angry. It isn't my fault. You're just a rotten kid. Blah, blah, blah.*

But clearly I'm a slow learner. An apology is the furthest thing from his mind. Why I should have thought such a thing was even possible shows what I fool I am.

"I brought extra work home," he says in explanation to my mother. "I didn't think it was safe to stay any later. None of us should be out after dark. The Negroes are burning down every big city in America."

At about a hundred thousand people, Lynn might be a big city compared to the cow pastures we used to live in up in Plainfield, Maine. It sure felt like the big, bad city when we moved here. But I hardly think Lynn qualifies as a big city on the national scale, and I haven't seen a single fire or even a fight today.

As if he's read my mind, my father adds, "We're no Boston or New York here, but this kind of thing spreads like wildfire. If the coloreds in this city aren't doing anything yet, they're going to get ideas from what they see on the television. Monkey see, monkey do. Mark my words. For at least the next few days, I don't want anyone outside of this house after dark. Doors locked. Shades drawn."

He moves to the adjoining front room and pulls closed the drapes.

"I don't think—" my mother begins, but falls silent when my father whirls and glares at her. She says, "I'll check the back door."

At my father's direction, I go upstairs to close all the shades, then return to the front room where the TV is on and today's papers are on the coffee table in front of the couch. The headline in the evening paper, the *Daily Evening Item*, reads,

KING'S SLAYING TRIGGERS VIOLENCE

One picture shows the Lorraine Motel in Memphis where Dr. King was assassinated. Another shows the side view of a bloodied black man with the caption: *Violence Victim—An unidentified man with blood streaming down his face, enters Boston City Hospital after being injured in the predominantly Negro Roxbury section of Boston by stone-throwing gangs who took to the streets following the death of Dr. Martin Luther King.*

Another headline reads *Police Stoned As Armed Negroes Roam Roxbury.* The stories tell of fires, looting, and the fatal stabbing of a white man in Washington, DC, and a possibly unrelated one of a black man in New York. A white youth died in a Florida fire started by a firebomb.

I read the stories in mounting horror, a sick feeling in the pit of my stomach. I understand the anger and hopelessness, but the violence could not be any more opposite to Dr. King's own beliefs. It's such a tragic, cruel irony that a great man who preached non-violence has been killed in the most violent act of all, and that act has triggered so much more violence.

Awful. Just awful.

I read another front page article of a ceremony on the Lynn Common to be held Sunday afternoon commemorating Dr. King.

It will begin with a march to the common and then end with the laying of a wreath at City Hall.

I gulp. My heart pounds.

I have to go. I have to be part of this. I have to show my support.

But will white people even be welcome? Will I be told to go away? Will I be stabbed to death?

I'm sure I won't be stabbed to death. These are Civil Rights leaders planning this march and tribute, certainly believers in Dr. King's message of non-violence, not angry gang members. But even Dr. King himself couldn't always control those who marched with him. Violence broke out sometimes. Often provoked, but still violence. In fact, he had returned to Memphis determined that this next march of his—one that now will never happen—would be unlike his previous march there in which violence did break out.

So yes, this might be a risk. Not an insanely foolish one, though. This isn't the South. It isn't Memphis. Or Andrew Goodman and Michael Schwerner traveling to Mississippi to help James Chaney register black voters, and paying for their courage with their lives. It isn't even Boston's black neighborhood of Roxbury.

It's a risk I've got to take.

My father isn't going to like this.

*

The images on the black-and-white TV almost make me change my mind.

Mom has made another exception to her rule about eating dinner together in the dining room. She and I are sitting together on the sofa, while my father is in the tan lounge chair cocked at a slight angle beside it. Plates of barely eaten American Chop Suey are before us on TV trays. We're all on the edge of our seats, riveted by what we're watching in horror.

It's one thing to read it in the newspaper, like I've just done. It's another to see it with your own eyes, narrated by Walter Cronkite. Flames rise high from buildings that will soon be nothing but ashes. Looters, almost exclusively young black men, pour in and out of stores, emerging with TV sets, radios, clothes, and liquor. Helmeted white policemen chase after black men and beat them with their nightsticks. The riots are happening in almost every big city in America.

"Lawless animals," my father predictably says, gesturing at the screen. "What did I tell you? They're burning their own neighborhoods down! Stealing from their own businesses."

Mom and I just watch in horror at this violation of everything Dr. King stood for. Even though the images are only in black and white, they could not appear any more real. I can almost feel the heat of the flames, smell the smoke, and taste on my lips the soot wafting through the air. And when another policeman's nightstick comes down on a black man's head or shoulders, my own head rings and the stab of pain shoots through me.

"I'm not stupid," my father says at the first break. "I know what the two of you think of me. You act like I'm some kind of prehistoric caveman who isn't blessed with your modern enlightenment and superior intelligence. You and your goody-two-shoes friends think that *everyone* is alike and the only difference between the Negroes and us is that we have money and they haven't been given a fair chance." He gestures angrily at the screen. "Well, who are the fools now? Do you think this is how white people would act?"

I want to argue that we have no way of understanding the pent-up rage of unjustly treated black people and their sudden explosion of fury, but I don't get the chance. The commercial ends, Walter Cronkite returns, and miraculously, Dear Old Dad shuts up.

In a video clip far less riveting than the riots, President Johnson somberly calls for peace to honor Dr. King's memory. The president, referred to by his initials, LBJ, in the newspaper headlines, looks horribly old with his thin hair and grandfather-style glasses. It's a video we've all seen multiple times.

Then, a new clip of Dr. King's final speech plays. He dismisses the importance of longevity, and talks about God allowing him, like the Biblical Moses, to go to a mountaintop.

"I've looked over, and I've seen the Promised Land," Dr. King says. "I may not get there with you. But I want you to know tonight, that we, as a people, will get to the Promised Land."

Chills run up and down my spine. My jaw drops. Mom and I look at each other in astonishment. It's as if Dr. King *knew* he was about to be assassinated.

Which is what Walter Cronkite says, noting that Dr. King had been subject to death threats for quite some time. And yet he didn't let them stop him. Like so many others involved in this righteous cause, he was willing to die for it.

My throat grows tight and my hands clammy. My heart pounds.

No matter how much the images of rioting scare me, and no matter what my father says, I *will* go on Sunday to that memorial service.

*

"*You what?*" my father says when I announce my intentions. He looks at me as if I'm an alien from outer space.

Mom looks astonished, too. Mouth open. Eyebrows raised.

"I want to pay tribute to Dr. King and what he stood for," I say. "It's important—"

"That service isn't for white people," my father says.

"It's for people who believe in Dr. King's ideals. White or black. If I go and they tell me they don't want me there, I'll leave. But I'm going."

My father gestures at the TV.

"Haven't you been paying attention? They might not tell you to go home. They might just stab you to death."

"White people marched with Dr. King," I say. "And I'm going to march on Sunday."

"Over my dead body!" my father says.

As if that would break my heart.

I don't really mean that, of course. It *would* break my heart, especially when I consider how things used to be between us. But if he could say out loud what he said this morning, then I can at least think this evil thought.

"Talk to your son!" he says to Mom. "Talk some sense into him."

*Talk to your son.* Has my father forgotten my name?

Mom takes a deep breath. She tilts her head back so her chin sticks out.

"I'll go with him," she says. "If I feel it's dangerous, we'll leave."

"*Whaaat?*" my father says, his eyes bulging out and his voice rising in pitch to that of a little girl's. "A woman in the middle of all those—?" He stops and tries again. "Both of you? I can't believe what I'm hearing!"

"Rabbit and I both believed in Dr. King's goals—"

"He was a communist!"

"We believed in his goals," Mom says with a firmness I've rarely heard from her. "A part of me wishes I could have marched with him down South, despite the dangers. That can't happen now, but Rabbit and I can march here on Sunday in support of what he believed in."

My father stares in open-mouthed astonishment.

"Didn't the two of you learn anything from the basketball protests? You both could have been injured seriously or even killed."

"If white thugs show up wearing ski masks and carrying sawed-off baseball bats," I say, "we'll be ready."

"Don't be a smart aleck!" my father snaps. "I simply won't allow it. I forbid it. End of story." He slices his hand through the air, which is his way of saying the discussion is over.

But then his eyes turn to Mom, and his shoulders slump. I can see that he remembers trying to order Mom to stop participating in the basketball protests, but she said that she would not be ordered around. She would follow her conscience.

"I don't mean *forbid*," he adds hastily. "I…I…" He shakes his head. "Marie, surely you can see the danger." He throws his hands out wide. "What do I have to do, march with the two of you just to make sure you're safe?"

"That sounds like a great idea!" Mom says brightly.

Astonished silence falls. I stare at her, and wonder if she's toying with my father or really means it. Surely she can't mean it. The image of my father, the bigot, joining a march in memory of Dr. King strikes me alternately as sacrilegious and hilarious. Mostly sacrilegious. My father has no business tarnishing with his racism what will be almost a sacred moment.

But imagining his discomfort as he's surrounded by hundreds, or more likely thousands, of black people is a treat more delicious than anything a world-class chef could ever cook up. I have to keep a smile from creeping onto my face. It might actually change his view of black people just a little—*wow, they're actually human beings like everyone else!*—but not even in my wildest imagination can I see it happening.

"I'll do no such thing," my father says indignantly. "I wasn't serious."

"But you should!" Mom says.

# CHAPTER 10

I never thought it would happen. Sunday arrives and my father is here with Mom and me outside the Gaylord Inter-Community Association building on Blossom Street, ready to march in memory of Dr. King. It's half past noon, and the march begins at one. Gaylord's is a two-story brick building, the long side of which angles away from the street, and has about twenty parking spots facing the building and then another twenty-five or so pointing out to the street. Cars of all make and model fill each spot.

Except for us, the growing crowd of three hundred people or so, most of them black but not all, are gathered in the middle of the lot. They've broken up into groups of five and ten, surrounded in front and back by the parked cars. My parents and I stand by ourselves beneath the shade of a thirty-foot-tall maple tree on a thin grassy strip at the far end of the lot. I can't help but feel my father has segregated us on the grass as far away from the others as possible, and I wish we could mingle with everyone else, but he insists we stay right where we are, as much on the outskirts as possible. Not just because he's afraid of all these black people, although that certainly doesn't help. Without even realizing he's doing it, he keeps patting his wallet that he moved from a back pants pocket to the front, apparently worried about pickpockets. But even more than that, he's terrified of any photographers who might take our picture and put it in the paper.

"That would really cause me problems at work," he says, as his eyes dart nervously about. "I'm here to watch out for you two, but God help me if my bosses find out about this." He shakes his head. "God help me."

Two police cruisers are parked on the sidewalk, their blue flashers pulsing. The smell of car fumes, hot asphalt, and whiffs of perfume fill the air. One cop directs traffic while another half dozen policemen—all of them white except one tall, broad-shouldered black man—are spread out on the sidewalk around all of us, moving about with nervous energy as if they're expecting a riot to break out.

But what's happening today isn't what we've been seeing on TV, entire city blocks burning to the ground, looters pilfering goods out of stores, and angry mobs hurling stones and bricks at police. What's happening today isn't what we've been reading in the newspapers, almost twenty people dead in the rioting, the National Guard and Army units called out to control the violence, with Chicago, Baltimore, and Washington, DC, particularly hard hit.

Instead, the mood here is somber and mournful with many exchanging tight-lipped handshakes or sorrowful hugs. Almost everyone is dressed for a funeral, which in many ways this is. The women are wearing dark-colored dresses, the men, dark suits and ties. I'm no fan of suits and I absolutely hate ties. I feel like my neck is being strangled whenever I wear one. But today I'm wearing a suit and tie without complaint.

While the cops are nervous but are trying to hide it, my father looks downright terrified. He gulps hard, and checks the knot of his tie. He bites his bottom lip, checks his wallet, and presses his black-rimmed glasses to the bridge of his nose. His heart has to be pounding harder, much harder, than in the old days back up in Maine—less than a year ago, but it feels like forever—when I'd coax him into playing one-on-one basketball with me. Or instead of him just standing there in the backyard throwing the football to me, I'd get him to lumber out for passes I'd throw to him. He isn't huffing and puffing now, gasping for breath, but I'm guessing his heart is pumping harder than it has in a long time.

Of course, he isn't here to memorialize Dr. King like everyone else is. He's here, ever so reluctantly, to "protect" Mom and me, although how he figures he could ever do that is a mystery. Out of shape and never an athlete, he has never held a weapon in his hands and may have never even thrown a punch. What could he possibly do to protect Mom and me?

But he's here, so I guess I have to give him credit for that. In fact, I've definitely got to give him credit for that.

He and I have had so many problems with each other since moving down here. I'm not about to forget that hard, back-handed slap that gave me a black eye just a couple weeks ago. Or the angry words. Or how at times he's seemed to actually hate both me and Mom.

But he's here today. Terrified out of his skin, but he's here.

Because he loves us.

*He still loves me.*

If that weren't true, he wouldn't be here. It wouldn't make sense. He loves me in spite of everything I do that exasperates him. He loves Mom in spite of her sticking up for me.

Beneath his ugly surface of bigotry and blind obsession for his job, beneath his explosions of anger at me when I misbehave—or when he thinks I misbehave—beneath all that, he's a good man, albeit one with some really bad faults, and a father who cares for his family.

I believe that. I have to believe it, I just have to.

Even if a part of me shakes its head at that naïve delusion—*you probably still believe in Santa Claus and the Easter bunny, too!—* and is sure I'm believing in my father's underlying goodness—*his goodness? really?*—only because it's what I want to believe. I'm just clinging to a tattered and faded remnant of the way things used to be back in the good old days, back before we moved and everything changed between him and me.

Maybe any goodness in my father has become buried so deep in the muck of what his life has become that it can never be extracted.

Maybe it isn't even there.

But I've got to believe it is. And moments like this extract it from the muck. I need to cling to that hope.

It's been a long time since I've thought of him as *Dad,* except to sarcastically refer to him as *Dear Old Dad.* He's just been…*my father.* Cold. Impersonal. Distant. He's deserved nothing better.

But his presence here makes me wonder about that, even as the wounds of his retracted words—*see if I care!*—are still fresh, barely scabbed over. Maybe our problems have been all my fault, or at least mostly my fault, after all. It hasn't felt like that at the time, but I wonder now if our problems haven't been as clearly black and white—all his fault except for my big mouth—as I've thought.

Maybe things are a lot more complicated than that. I don't know.

But I know that he's here because he loves me. And he loves Mom.

I'm not quite ready to think of him as *Dad.* The icy coldness between us hasn't quite thawed out that much. But for the first time in what feels like forever, I sense the embers of my past love for him, so long buried beneath such a mountain of hatred and resentment that I'd thought they'd been forever extinguished. And those embers are beginning to glow.

*

While we've been waiting for the march to begin, many of the black people in attendance, especially several of those who appear to be the leaders, have approached us, thanked us for coming, and shaken our hands. One barrel-chested man even gave my father a hug, which surely had to be a first. I can only imagine what my father was thinking when that happened.

But we haven't approached anyone ourselves. We've stuck to the outskirts of the group, feeling a bit like the outsiders that in many ways we are, despite the welcoming efforts of so many of those here. I had hoped to see Charlie, Jessie, Jamaal, or any of my other black friends here, but none of us has recognized a single face.

My father spots several white men and women at the opposite end of the parking lot, and seems to breathe a sigh of relief.

"We can't stay under this tree all day," he whispers to Mom. "The march will be starting soon enough. Maybe we should to go over and introduce ourselves." He nods in the direction of a white couple, who are probably in their mid-twenties, both dark-haired and of moderate height and weight.

"Do you know them?" Mom asks, not moving.

"No, that's why I said we should introduce ourselves," my father says, a bit exasperated as if it was a stupid question.

"Then we'll do no such thing," she says. "If we've stayed all the way over here away from everyone, and we haven't introduced ourselves to the black people here—"

"That's because we don't *belong* here. This is *their* march, *their* service."

"Since we haven't introduced ourselves to the black people here, instead waiting for them to come to us, then we're not going to do anything different with white people who are here."

"But—"

"Because if we go over there, we'll almost certainly stay there talking with them. Next thing you know—unless you're suggesting we mingle and also introduce ourselves to all the black people we haven't spoken with yet—there'll be a white section of the crowd distinct from the black section. And the whites will wind up marching together, and a march intended to honor Dr. King will wind up as segregated as Alabama and Mississippi."

My father's face turns stony for a time, then goes slack.

"Okay," he finally says. "I see your point."

And so, the crowd remains integrated, grains of salt mixed in with pepper, as the somber march heads up Blossom Street, escorted by one of the police cruisers, its blue flashers strobing. Everyone marches hand-in-hand, ten astride, the three of our family in the middle of a row that's close to the back. I'm between my mother and father, who are holding the hands of black people they never knew before today. My father has settled down somewhat, but remains nervous, looking all about for danger, his palm clammy and sweaty in my own, his grip tight, almost to the point of discomfort. I wonder if the black man whose hand he is holding notices.

We turn left onto Summer Street, and then down Vine. As we do, people along those streets who have been waiting for the march to get to them—perhaps worried that there could be violence, but now reassured—join the hundreds of us who began back at Gaylord's.

On Neptune Street, I'm delighted to see Charlie Watkins and his mother emerge from the three-story, three-family house they live in and blend in with the rest of the growing crowd.

*

I separate myself from my parents to walk beside Charlie. Like me, he's wearing a dark suit, white shirt, tie, and polished dress shoes. We've never seen each other dressed up like this, so we check each other out appreciatively.

"You ain't half ugly," Charlie says, and we laugh, momentarily forgetting the solemnity of the occasion.

Charlie's mother, who is wearing a black dress and a necklace with a cross on it, gives me an affectionate pat on the cheek, then melts into a row ahead of us to be with friends she's spotted. Also, I'm sure, to let us be alone. Charlie's now on the outside of a row. I'm to his left. Unlike the adults around us, we don't hold hands. That would feel weird.

"Why am I not surprised to see you here?" Charlie asks.

"Had to be here, man," I say. "Had to."

Charlie nods. Both of our grins are gone. The reason we're here has settled over us.

"Coach Kowalski right about one thing," Charlie says. "You a rebel."

"Proud of it."

Out of nowhere, I think of the cartoon character Popeye saying, "I yam what I yam." And maybe that's all it comes down to. A year ago, I was a kid who thought about nothing but sports. That's who I was. Now, if there's a cause I believe in, I feel compelled to stand up for it. That's who I am.

I yam what I yam.

"My momma has problems with her knee," Charlie says, "so she figured we could join up with the march here, save about half the walking."

I nod. "Makes sense."

"She'll never admit it, but I also think she wanted to see if there was trouble," Charlie says. "Scary stuff on the TV. Sad stuff. Probably the reason there aren't thousands here now."

I nod. "I had to drag my parents here. When I said I was gonna march, my father went through the roof. So my mom said she'd look after me, get me to leave if it seemed there might be trouble."

"She cool," Charlie says, nodding, clearly remembering her role in the basketball protests.

"My father was scared stiff of what might happen here, but he couldn't get us to change our minds. So he got cornered into joining us, too." I shake my head. "Trust me, he don't want to be here. At...all."

"Had the impression he ain't exactly sympathetic to the cause."

"That's putting it mildly."

"Well, my momma would say you brought a sinner to the revival meeting," Charlie says. "Let's see if he gets saved."

I ponder the impossibility of that miracle and just shake my head.

"Ain't gonna happen," I say.

We walk a short while before Charlie says, "You hear what happened to Jessie?"

A sliver of fear shoots through me. "No, what?"

"He and his girlfriend, Rose, was supposed to go to the James Brown concert at the Garden last night. Had tickets and everything. 'Cept with all the looting and fires and stuff, his parents said he couldn't go. Just wasn't safe. Man, he was really upset."

"I can imagine," I say.

"But Channel 2 televised the concert, so Rose goes over his house and they watching the concert and making out and stuff. Probably more making out than watching the concert," Charlie says with a short, rueful laugh. "So it's like they having a date anyway, and they dancing to a song when a rock or a brick or something like that gets thrown through their front room window. Almost hits them. Glass goes flying everywhere and they don't know if it a rock, a bomb, or a Molotov cocktail, and the house is about to burn down.

"Turns out, it was just a rock, 'bout the size of a football. But when the cops get there, and everyone look outside, they see a message spray-painted on the house: NEGROES, GO AWAY. Only the word wasn't Negroes."

*

It takes about an hour to cover the one-mile route. Slow, befitting a funeral march. A thick, dark cloud of sorrow blankets us all. For Charlie and me, there's the extra gut-wrenching news of what happened to Jessie to deepen our despair, but there's no shortage of heartache for everyone else. Tears stream down faces. Handkerchiefs dab at wet eyes. A few women sob out of control, horrible retching sounds that seize your heart in a tight-fisted grip and squeeze it, making it almost impossible to keep from joining in. Others show only stoic, stone faces, a mask for emotions that may include as much anger and resentment as grief. Grief and perhaps even resigned surrender, the cause now considered futile.

I had imagined the marchers would sing anthems associated with the Civil Rights movement and expected to sing along, but there's no singing and almost no talking. Charlie and I say little now, showing our respect for Dr. King in quiet contemplation.

The march stops at City Hall, and a wreath about two-thirds my size is laid at the base of the fifty-foot-high metal flagpole, where the flag hangs at half-mast. A red ribbon on the wreath provides a heartbreaking message: "I Have a Dream – We Shall Overcome."

By the time we get to the wooden bandstand on the Common, the somber crowd has grown to well over a thousand people. To be honest, I had thought there would be even more, but there's no discounting the fear generated by the recent TV images of burning cities. Perhaps I was naïve to blindly assume the peaceful rally we have experienced. I'd also expected the crowd to be almost exclusively black, but as it now surrounds the bandstand, it's far more racially balanced than I ever would have thought.

Metal folding chairs have been placed in front of and on both sides of the four long curving rows of permanent metal benches, but all together there isn't room for more than three or four hundred people to sit. The seats fill fast, so Charlie and I stand behind the back row of permanent benches, about sixty feet from the podium and twenty feet to the left of my parents. Others form additional standing rows behind us.

Leaning on the wooden handrails, dignitaries climb the side steps onto the wooden bandstand's platform, and take their seats behind a lectern and microphone stand. They're beneath a pointed roof supported by eight wooden columns atop a three-foot high circular wall of stone.

Mom turns and gets on her tiptoes to check on me for what is probably the hundredth time, smiles, and turns her attention to a speaker testing the microphone.

The service takes an hour. One speaker after another steps to the lectern, praises Dr. King and his sacrifice in pursuit of equality for all, then exhorts us to continue that fight against racism. The main speakers are black—one calls Dr. King "a gentle apostle of God…a fallen warrior"—but are followed by a succession of white ministers, priests, rabbis, and the mayor.

And then, just as I'm feeling restless at this succession of white men saying the same things the other white men before him have said, and I wonder how many of them have really offered anything more than mere words in support of racial equality, we hear a recording of Dr. King's most famous speech, the one known as "I Have a Dream."

Before it starts, we're encouraged to take the hand of the person next to us. On my left, I take the bony hand of a thin, mostly bald, elderly black man, hunched over with age and surely deserving of a seat to rest his weary bones. On my right, Charlie grasps my hand firmly, and now it isn't weird at all.

The hiss of static fills the air. While the sound quality is imperfect, the words that follow are unforgettable.

*"I have a dream that one day this nation will rise up and live out the true meaning of its creed: 'We hold these truths to be self-evident: that all men are created equal.'"*

I bow my head. My throat tightens. I think of what this great man accomplished, but how much remains to be done, and what his loss means to the dream of equality. And not just in the worst of Alabama and Mississippi, but up here in the North, too. And not just because of what happened to Jessie.

As Dr. King's static-filled speech continues, he speaks, in rising and falling cadences, of the descendants of former slaves and the descendants of former slave owners sitting together in brotherhood. And of his own small children one day being judged not by the color of their skin, but by the content of their character.

The phrase "content of their character" rings in my head. Will we ever see the day when people, not just in the South but also right here in Massachusetts, right here in Lynn, are judged not by their color, but by the content of their character? When will Charlie and Jessie be treated no differently than I am?

Dr. King's voice rings out, speaking of all people singing with true meaning, "My country 'tis of thee, sweet land of liberty."

All about me, people are weeping. Some call out, "Yes!" and "Amen!" On my left, the old man shouts, "Preach it, Martin! Preach it!"

I belatedly realize that tears are streaming down my own face, noticing it only when they reach my lips, tasting salty and bitter. A momentary flash of humiliation hits me. I'm crying in front of Charlie! But as I turn to try to explain, I see that his eyes are squeezed shut. He's shaking his head, and his face is contorted in pain.

The recording of Dr. King's speech finishes with its epic climax, his dream of the day when God's children of every race, creed, and religion can sing the words:

*"Free at last! Free at last! Thank God almighty, we are free at last!"*

Charlie grips my hand so tightly it hurts. His hand shakes with emotion.

A lump forms in my throat. My breath quickens.

Charlie and I are not alone in our reaction. Grief overtakes everyone around us. I happen to glance over at my parents.

And I see the most astonishing sight I have ever seen.

My father, head bowed and eyes squeezed tightly shut, lets go of my mother's hand so he can remove his glasses and dry his eyes. He isn't actually crying—no tears streak down his face like they do so many others, including Mom's—but he's clearly moved in a way I've never seen before. He presses the wrist of his black suit against his eyes, daubing them dry.

My jaw drops.

I can't believe what I'm seeing. I don't mean to stare, but I can't tear my eyes away from the sight. All the awful things my father has said about black people in the past flash through my mind: They're animals. They don't think like us. We should thank him because he bought us a house in the most lily-white neighborhood he could find. It's okay if they burn down their own neighborhoods.

Awful, awful words.

Now this.

It can't be true. Surely, I'm seeing what I want to see, once again acting like the astronomer Percival Lowell who, at the turn of the century, looked into his telescope and was so sure he saw canals on Mars, he mapped them out. Even though there were no canals and no Martians. He saw what he wanted to see.

I've got to be pulling a Percival Lowell now. There's no way my father has changed. Not like this.

But he has!

Charlie was right. The sinner came to the revival. The sinner got saved.

*

My father doesn't speak of it until we're alone in the car, Mom in front and me in back behind her. He doesn't start the car. He grips the steering wheel so tightly his knuckles turn white. He turns halfway around so he can look at both of us.

"I suppose I've been wrong about a few things," he says in a shaky voice. "Not everything," he adds quickly, "but some. A lot." He breathes noisily in through his nose. "Those black people there today…they weren't like the ones I've been reading about…like the ones I've been seeing on the TV. These seem to be reasonable, law-abiding, fair-minded people. The things I've said in the past… the things I've thought…well…I guess they don't apply to these people.

"And I'll admit that I've been afraid of Martin Luther King. Afraid of his marches and of the anger, however justified, of those who marched with him. But it's hard to listen to that speech of his and not…and not be moved by his dream, and not feel…

compassion for the plight of his people…and not feel just a horrible sense of regret for some of the things I've said and thought.

"Now if you want to say, 'I told you so,' then go right ahead. Rub my nose in it if you want. But I just never…I never…" He shakes his head. "I don't know…I just never saw things from that perspective. Never saw it through their eyes. I guess it took being around all of them, the men wearing suits and ties just like you and me, and the women in dresses like your mother, to realize…"

He stops, unable to finish the sentence. The car falls quiet.

So I finish the sentence for him. "They're just like us."

He opens his mouth to argue the point. The sinner might have gotten saved, but a lot of the old sin still lurks in his heart. He sits motionless for what feels like forever.

"I don't know if I'd say that," he says finally. "Some of them on the TV burning down their own neighborhoods, and looting TVs out of the stores…" He shakes his head. "I don't think those people are like us. Not at all."

I consider trying to explain, as best as a stupid white kid can, what I understand as the reasons for the rage that has led to the cities burning. But what do I really know about what it's like to be black? What do I know about how a black person feels? Anything I say would sound both pretentious and patronizing. And might blow up in my face with my father taking back almost everything he's just said. I need to quit while we're ahead.

So for once in my life, I keep my big mouth shut.

"But those people we marched with today," my father says, nodding, with a faraway look in his eyes. "Those were good people."

It may not be the most perfect, one-hundred-percent conversion of a race-relations sinner, but it's close. It's still a miracle.

# CHAPTER 11

When my father comes down to breakfast the next morning, he's dressed for work in his usual black suit, white shirt, and tie. Like always, he sits to my left at the head of the table while Mom bustles about in the kitchen. And as he so often does, he slurps his hot coffee until it cools. But everything else about him feels different.

The outside is the same. The inside is different.

It's not like he's suddenly an imitation of Dr. King himself, an enlightened ambassador for racial equality. And it's not like he's suddenly the Dad of old back up in Maine. Tonight, we're not going out into the backyard to play catch until the mosquitoes carry us off to Canada. And who knows if that backhanded slap of his is still lurking in the dark shadows, waiting to give me another black eye.

But he's different.

*Really* different, and in a good way. A great way, actually.

It's as if admitting he was wrong about black people has somehow allowed him to act as if he was wrong about other things—about *us*, about *me*—without actually having to say so out loud. Or maybe it's that he respects me more, he *has* to respect me more—both me *and* Mom, actually—since we were so right about Dr. King and black people, and he was so wrong.

I don't know. I'm no Sigmund Freud. I can't explain the change in him from night to day.

All I know is that as we eat Mom's breakfast of pancakes and scrambled eggs—both of them hot and steaming, the butter on the pancakes melting quickly and filling the air with a buttery smell to go along with the sweet maple scent of the syrup—my father for once doesn't bury his head in the newspaper.

He actually talks to me. And even better, he listens to what I say.

"I know that the mayor has declared tomorrow a day of mourning because of the funeral for Martin Luther King—Dr. King," he says. "One of the speakers yesterday suggested that everyone stay home from work or school as part of the day of mourning." My father shifts uncomfortably in his chair. "I, um…I can't do that. My position at work isn't like that. I can't just fail to show up. My vacations have to be scheduled well ahead of time and coordinated with a few of the other managers so someone can cover for me and we're not all out at the same time. I can't just announce that tomorrow I'm not going to be there."

I nod, understanding.

"I know how you feel," he says. "If you think you should stay home from school, I'll support that. Your mother or I will sign a note approving your absence. I'd prefer that you go. I don't think staying home from school is the right tribute to what he—what Dr. King—stood for. But I'll leave that up to you."

My fork clatters to my plate. I stare at my father open-mouthed, subconsciously thankful I'd finished chewing and swallowing my last mouthful of pancakes. For all I know, my eyes are bugging out at this strange sight. I can't believe my father's transformation.

Since when does he leave decisions like this—heck, *any* decisions—up to me? What has happened to the man who felt obligated to dictate my every move? Who didn't trust me to make good decisions by myself. The man with whom I was constantly at war?

"Thanks," I say, and I really am grateful for this show of trust. "I'll think about it."

He mentions the rioting—which has killed twenty-four people, almost all of them black—calming down in most of the big cities. I relate what happened at Jessie's house, the rock getting thrown through the front window and the spray-painting of that awful message.

My father recoils in shock. He shakes his head in dismay.

"That's awful!" he says. "I hope they catch whoever did it, and lock them up!"

I briefly wonder what his reaction to what happened would have been just a few days ago, but then push that thought out of my mind. He's changed and that's what matters.

So instead of provoking my father with some caustic remark, I mention that the rock crashed through the front window while Jessie and his girlfriend, Rose, were watching the telecast of the James Brown concert at the Garden.

"James Brown? Really?" my father replies, pausing to take another bite of pancakes. "The running back for the Cleveland Browns? He retired only two or three years ago. And he's already a successful musician?"

I blink, then laugh so hard I almost choke on my scrambled eggs. I laugh uncontrollably even as my father stares at me, befuddled at my merriment. I suppose I'm not being fair. Six months ago, I probably wouldn't have known the difference either. I didn't know *anything* about black music. As far as I can tell, none of it ever played up in Maine. Everybody was white up there and nobody listened to black music.

I still know only a tiny bit about it, mostly from talking to Charlie, Jamaal, and Jessie. Since I'm sure there isn't a single black person my father ever talks to, his ignorance of a singer of James Brown's stature is understandable. But it still hits me squarely in the funny bone.

"James Brown, the Godfather of Soul," I finally say, still laughing. "Not the running back. That's a different guy. The running back went by 'Jim.' *Jim* Brown."

"Oh," my father says, his face flushing momentarily with embarrassment. "Yeah, Jim Brown. That's it." Then he adds, defensively, "Although I'm sure it's James Brown on his birth certificate."

*His birth certificate?*

This gets me howling even more. I suppose I should be concerned that my father is going to show his displeasure at my making fun of him, and maybe even give me a wallop. I should really knock it off. With things between us suddenly so good, I shouldn't risk blowing it all apart.

But saying "I'm sure it's James Brown on his birth certificate" is such a cluelessly Dad thing to say. I just can't help myself.

Besides, this isn't that same man who slapped me so hard he knocked me off my chair and gave me a black eye. Not the same at all. Somehow, I just know my black-eye days are over. At least, I sure hope so.

And sure enough, what comes next isn't a slap on the face for being disrespectful. He breaks into laughter, too. Soft and embarrassed at first, but then harder and louder.

I try to think when the last time was that we laughed together. And I'm stumped. I can't remember it.

I can remember the last shouting match. The last words of pure, unadulterated hatred. And of course, that last backhanded slap.

But the last shared laughter? I'll have to pull that one up from the memory banks and dust it off. I can only hope that golden oldie felt as good as this one.

And unless I'm crazy or self-deluded—always a real possibility with me—I see a warm pleasure in my father's face at our laughter. And a quick glance at Mom makes that three of us.

Good times for all.

And I suddenly realize he's no longer just "my father."

He's "Dad" again.

*Dad!*

Maybe I'm jumping the gun. Maybe it'll fall apart. Maybe what I perceive as him changing is all a matter of wish fulfillment.

Maybe there's no happy ending.

But it sure feels like everything is different. *Dad.* Before, it was a term he didn't deserve. Now, it's one that, at least tentatively, I'm going to use. Because he's earned it.

*Dad.*

It feels so strange to use that word again, even if only in my mind.

It feels wonderful. Magical, almost.

After all these months of fighting, of dealing with Mutually Assured Destruction if we let loose on each other the worst of our bombs, he's now *Dad* again. A probationary Dad, but still…

*Dad.*

Suddenly fear stabs me in the heart. A fear I can't ignore. I can tell myself it won't happen anymore, but I need to *know.*

I can't wonder. I have to know.

It's the one thing that could blow all of this into smithereens. The one danger that could tear us apart all over again. Push Humpty Dumpty off the wall, and the pieces will never, ever fit back together again.

Should I play it safe? Quit while I'm ahead? Just enjoy the happiness for at least a day, at least an hour, *at least a minute* before putting it to the test?

But have I ever played it safe? Have I ever used caution before opening my big mouth?

No.

And so like a base runner flying into third with a standup triple who thinks he can maybe, just maybe, turn it into an inside-the-park home run, I decide to go for it. With my heart pounding and my mind screaming at me that I'm going to ruin it all, I make the mad dash for home.

"*Dad?*" I ask cautiously.

His eyes widen in surprise. He takes in a quick, audible gulp of air. He's noticed the word. *Dad.* I haven't used it for months. He's noticed its absence. Months that have felt like years, maybe for him just like for me. Maybe what happened to us has hurt him as much as it's hurt me, even if he hasn't shown it.

"What, Rabbit?" he asks, his voice uncertain.

He blinks, faster and faster. It almost looks like his eyes are watering, and he's blinking away the tears. Could it be?

I think it is.

He gulps, and leans forward expectantly.

I look over at Mom. The blood rushes from her face as she stares at me, no doubt wondering how I'm going to foul things up now.

Suddenly, I can barely breathe. It seems like all three of us are holding our breaths.

"Could I ask one thing?" I say. "It would mean a lot. I don't want you to get angry, but—"

His face flushes. His jaw sets. "What?"

I've gone and done it now. I've done it again. Pushed too far. I've snatched defeat from the jaws of victory. Opened my big mouth when I should have kept it shut.

But it's too late to turn back now. I've passed the point of no return. And so I blurt out the words before I change my mind.

"Can you promise never to hit me again?"

He recoils, and rocks back in his seat. looking like this time he's the one who's been slapped. Mom gasps and puts a hand to her mouth.

Dad's face reddens even more than before. A lot more.

I wonder if this signals an upcoming explosion. In fact, I'm sure it does. I've gone too far. I even know what he's going to say. *Don't you tell me what to do, young man.* And then he'll be off and running about how sparing the rod spoils the child. And it's turned me into a spoiled brat.

"Punish me if I deserve it," I say quickly, trying to repair the damage even though I know it's too late. "I'm not telling you what to do. I know you're the boss. Take away my privileges. Make me do more chores. Whatever you have to do.

"Just don't hit me. Don't hit me so hard you knock me to the floor. Don't…don't make me have to put on makeup when I go to school to cover up a black eye."

I break into tears. I try to stop, but I can't. Horrible wracking sobs overtake my body. I duck my head in shame. I'm bawling like a baby, and I can't stop. Salty tears run onto my lips. Snot runs down my nose.

I feel Dad's hand on my shoulder. Giving it a squeeze. Mom comes around behind me, and I smell her talcum powder and clean soap as she leans over and wraps her arms around me.

"Rabbit?" Dad says, still sitting but leaning forward.

I look through blurry, tear-filled eyes. I grab a napkin that's next to my fork. It's sticky with syrup, so I fold it over and wipe the snot from my nose.

Dad's lips quiver. Tears fill his eyes. He looks down at the table, then back up at me.

"I regret that. I do now," Dad says, nodding. "But you scare me sometimes. You've changed so much in the last year. It's like you're a different person.

"You're a good kid—a great kid—but you have such a rebellious streak in you. As a parent, it's my job to keep that under control. And controlling you is like…controlling a tornado. I don't know what to do with you sometimes." He looks down at his hands. "I feel as though I've lost control, and if I'm not careful, your rebellion will spin wildly out of control, and I'll wind up visiting you in a jail someday.

"It's my duty as a parent, my obligation to you, to keep you from going bad." He shrugs. "So I've done what my father did to keep me in line when I was a teenager. He'd read me the riot act, and when that wasn't enough, he'd give me a smack. I didn't like it, but I stopped doing what I'd been doing.

"So I just thought…well…I don't know what I thought. It just seemed like that's the way it's always been done, and I thought that's the way it should be."

With my heart in my throat, I hope with everything I have that Dad doesn't add, *And that's the way it's going to be. And if you don't like it, that's just too bad.*

But he doesn't say that. Not at all. He studies his hands, perhaps wondering what caused them to hit me, and shakes his head. Then says the best words ever.

"I'll never hit you again," he says. "I thought I was doing what was right for you. To keep you in control. To keep you a good kid. Keep you on the straight and narrow. I was angry at you, sure. Really angry. So maybe…maybe it was a lot easier to do than it should have been. But I thought I was just doing my job as a parent. I guess I was wrong about that, too.

"So I promise. Never again."

I know he means it. I know in the depths of my heart that he'll honor that promise. This isn't something he's just saying.

He stands up, his chair noisily skidding on the linoleum floor, and moves next to me. I stand up and we hug, Dad from in front, and Mom from behind. We hug hard, as if holding on for dear life.

A sense of purest joy and peace fills me all over. We're finally a family again.

For once in my life, I'm thankful I opened my big mouth.

# CHAPTER 12

The next day, Tuesday morning, I meet Anna at her locker, and she's still beaming over the family news I related to her the previous morning. That my father and I somehow put our fractured relationship back together again. From Mutually Assured Destruction to…a family again! When I told her, she wrapped her arms around me and cried tears of pure joy. We hugged for so long with her telling me over and over how happy she was for me, it's amazing we didn't get in trouble with one of the teachers.

Today, we're both still walking on clouds. *A family again!* It's hard to believe. And Anna, pretty as ever in her dark blue dress with white trim, her brown eyes sparkling behind her glasses, is almost as happy for me as I am for myself. We're all smiles and laughter.

Until we see a black classmate.

Fortunately, we see Janice Downing before she sees us. In the sparse hallway traffic, she's walking alone on the other side, wearing a pretty black dress, her eyes downcast. Anna and I fall suddenly silent and our smiles freeze as we remember that today is the day of mourning for Dr. King and for his funeral. Suddenly, our glee, as well deserved as it may be, feels terribly inappropriate and disrespectful.

By the time Janice glances our way, we're both looking appropriately somber. I give a nod and a tight smile in greeting and Anna gives a little wave. Janice nods back then looks quickly away.

I'm actually surprised any of us are here. I had thought the city would cancel school in observance of the day of mourning. After all, the Celtics postponed their playoff game, as have most of the other sports teams. Everything else seems to have shut down to pay respect to Dr. King. But not the city and not Lynn English.

Unfortunately, as it turns out.

Since the traffic in the hallways is lighter than usual, we see Charlie coming as soon as he pushes through the fire doors forty feet down the corridor. A look of grim sadness covers his face. Perhaps it's coincidental that he's dressed all in black—a black, button-down shirt and black pants—but I don't think so.

"Figured you'd be here," he says to me with a slight grin that's there and gone so fast I'm not sure it was ever there at all. "Sorry to interrupt."

"It's okay," Anna and I both say at the same time. Usually we'd grin after saying something like that in unison, but not today. The sadness in Charlie's eyes offers a reminder of the day's solemnity that we don't need. His shoulders seem to sag with the weight of sorry and perhaps even defeat.

"Most of the brothers ain't here today," he says. "Only Jessie, me, and on the varsity, J.P. Clayton. From the team, I mean. I don't want to be here, but I skipped yesterday, and my momma says I can't miss both days.

"But I sure don't think it's right that we expected to play a baseball game on the day of Dr. King's funeral. Practically during it. Bad enough the city don't cancel school today. Bad enough we had to play our game on Friday. I get that everything was just crazy that day, and everything was happening so fast, and no one knew what to do.

"But man, today's a day of mourning. The day of his funeral! There's no excuse for not cancelling or postponing today's game." Charlie shakes his head. "It's disrespectful. Not spit-on-someone's-grave disrespectful, but disrespectful anyway. Just acting as if nothing important has happened. Maybe give us some token moment of silence before the game starts and think that's enough.

"Well it ain't. The Celtics postponed their playoff game from Sunday to Wednesday. A NBA playoff game! Three days! Major league baseball's moving back all their season openers. But the Merrimack Valley League can't postpone a high school game that maybe fifty people coming to watch? The Celtics can postpone a playoff game for three days, but high school baseball's too important?"

I nod vigorously. I hadn't even thought about today's game. I've known since the schedule came out that we had a game today. We play almost every Tuesday and Friday. My clean uniform is in my gym locker, like always, but my mind has been in such a daze that I haven't put two and two together. Dr. King's death and everything that has happened since then have pushed baseball so far into the background that it almost isn't even there.

"It ain't right," Charlie says. "So the brothers here today ain't gonna play. Same with Hector Martinez and José Fernandez. Guess you could call it a boycott. We ain't playing. So that's eleven guys either ain't here today or not playing.

"So Kowalski ain't gonna have a choice. You gonna get your shot. All those guys missing, he's got to play you on JVs."

I'm an idiot for not even thinking about this. For not connecting Dr. King's funeral and the day of mourning with the baseball game.

"I'm gonna boycott, too," I say, instinctively.

Charlie winces.

"Was afraid you might say that," he says, and shakes his head sadly. "Don't do it. It's the right thing, but it's the wrong thing, if you know what I mean. You do that, you're finished with Kowalski. He already hate you cause of what you said. You boycott this game with us, it'll confirm everything bad about you he ever suspected.

You just the troublemaker he was sure you was even before you opened your mouth. You might as well give your glove and cleats to Anna here. You ain't never playing for the varsity or JVs. He might even kick you off the freshmen team."

Everything Charlie says makes sense. He's right. Right as rain, my mom would say.

"I hear you, man," I say, "but how can I play? I gotta support you guys. Nobody should be playing today, white or black."

Charlie nods.

"I'll tell the guys we got your support," he says. "You was ready to boycott, and I talked you out of it. Because I gotta talk you out of it. This is your shot, man. Your chance to show Kowalski he's wrong about you. Your chance to force him to keep you on JVs once you play there and show your stuff. Get three hits, steal four bases, and score each time you get on. He can't send you back to the freshmen team after that."

I nod numbly, my mind a jumble of contradictory thoughts. Charlie's right about Kowalski. This would burn every last bridge with him down to the ground. Burn it down, then spit on the ashes.

But this is also a matter of right and wrong. I can't use Dr. King's death as my "opportunity." If it's disrespectful for the school to play the game, then it's disrespectful for me to be a part of it. I can't rationalize that away. I don't *want* to rationalize it away. I'm not going to sell my soul for the chance to play JVs.

"I can't do it," I say. "I just can't."

"You got to," Charlie says. "That's why I came here this morning, 'cause I know you and I know how you think. I know you want to support us. You always want to be part of a righteous cause. But this one time, let us fight our own battle. You boycott today's game with us, Kowalski's gonna bury you forever. Forever! Maybe he accept us brothers boycotting cause we black. But you white. You boycott, and you just a troublemaker. Like he think you is anyway."

I say nothing. I know Charlie's right. There's not even a question in my mind about it. But I still can't imagine playing. I'd feel like I sold my friends out, and sold out the cause.

I swallow hard and shake my head. "Can't do it. I'd feel like a traitor."

"You got to play!" he says.

I shrug helplessly. I'd tell him I'll think about it, but my mind is already made up. I can't possibly play and feel right about it.

"Listen, I gotta run." He turns to Anna. "Try to talk some sense into that thick skull of his."

After he rushes off, Anna says, "He's probably right."

"He is," I say. "But I can't."

Anna nods sadly. She knew I was going to say that.

*

Coach Gilhooly is waiting for me outside my fourth period classroom, Science, when Anna and I approach it. Seeing him, she gives me a sad look, excuses herself. and ducks inside. He's wearing a blue button-down shirt and tan slacks, his short brown hair neatly parted on the side. He's smiling broadly, but I'm pretty sure I'm about to wipe the smile off his face.

"Great news, Rabbit!" he says as other students stream around us, talking and laughing. "You're finally getting your shot at the JVs today. I'm sure you'll do great." Perhaps reading something on my face, his smile freezes and then is gone. "What's the matter? This is the opportunity you've been waiting for."

"I'm only getting the opportunity because none of the black players are going to play today," I say. "Same with Hector and José. Because today is Dr. King's funeral. A day that is supposed to be a day of mourning."

"That is true," he says grudgingly. "We won't be able to field a freshmen team today because players on the JVs are moving up to varsity, and you and most of the other freshmen are moving up to fill all the holes on the JVs. But it's still a great opportunity to show that you belong on JVs. Don't look a gift horse in the mouth."

"We shouldn't be playing," I say.

A pained look comes to his face. His shoulders sag. "Don't tell me you aren't—"

"The Celtics postponed their playoff game out of respect to Dr. King," I say. "An NBA *playoff* game. But we can't show the same level of respect?"

Coach Gilhooly shrugs. "It's a league decision. We have to abide by that decision whether we like it or not."

"I'm sorry, Coach, but I can't play."

Coach Gilhooly stares at me like I'm a hopeless case. "Rabbit, you've *got* to play. It's your last chance. Listen, we both know you got off on the wrong foot with Coach Kowalski. I know you've been frustrated, and I understand that. But I also understand where he's coming from. He doesn't trust you. If you refuse to play today, it'll confirm that he *can't* count on you. You'll be committing baseball suicide. I'm begging you to reconsider."

"Coach, do I give everything I possibly can to the team? Is there anyone who works harder?"

"That isn't the point."

"This is a matter of principle," I say. "I'm sorry, but I can't play."

The bell rings for the next class to start. Coach Gilhooly shakes his head in disappointment.

"Think about it," he says. "I won't tell Coach Kowalski until you fail to show up. But I wouldn't do this if I were you. You're a very talented player with a bright future. I'd hate to see you ruin it with one bad decision."

And with that, he's gone.

I take my seat in the classroom, near the back on the left, about as far as possible from Anna, who's up close and on the right. I feel as glum as I can remember in a very long time. I'm trying to do the right thing, but everyone is telling me I shouldn't do it. It isn't so much the advice of Coach Gilhooly, who has a vested interest in me playing. Mostly, it's Charlie, telling me to pick a different battle to fight. And I suppose Anna's sad look of resignation when I told her I couldn't possibly play, and then again when she saw Coach Gilhooly outside the classroom.

But isn't acting on your principles *always* the right thing to do? What kind of person only sticks up for what is right when it's easy? When the price to be paid doesn't hurt? How will I feel about myself if I decide to discard my principles *just this one time* because my baseball future is at stake? Be a traitor to the cause because the price is too high?

Dr. King paid for his pursuit of racial justice *with his life*. But I'm supposed to consider playing for the JVs too high a cost to do the right thing?

I can't do it. Even if it means I never put on a Lynn English baseball jersey again. Even if it means I never play another competitive game of baseball.

The very thought makes me feel like I've been punched in the gut. *Never play another competitive game of baseball.* I almost feel nauseated. I've enjoyed so many great times on the baseball diamond. Diving on the infield dirt to snare a ground ball, then bouncing to my feet to throw the runner out at first base. Hearing the crack of my bat on the ball, sending a scorching liner into the gaps for a double or triple. Or getting just a single, but stealing second and third to turn it effectively into a triple. Or the simple pleasures of smelling the freshly cut grass and feeling the grit of the infield dirt beneath my fingernails. Hearing the infield chatter of, "Hey, batter. Hey, batter. Hey, batter."

The thought of losing all that makes me feel so sad I want to cry. I won't, of course, not here in my classroom seat, my arms on the beige tablet arm part of the desk, surrounded by close to thirty classmates, including Anna, pretending to pay attention to Mr. Tempkin talk about Science.

But I'd always thought that doing the right thing would feel better than this.

*

At lunch, I call my mom from the dark-stained wooden phone booth on the first floor, sliding a dime into the chrome-colored slot and speaking into the black handset. I tell her that I won't be playing today because of Dr. King's funeral. I don't say that I'm *choosing* not to play, just that there's no need for her to come watch the game. Some things are better explained in person than on the phone. I offer to take the bus home, but she says she'll pick me up anyway. Whether it's because of the problems I had with Smitty on the bus at the beginning of the school year or that she's gotten to like the conversations we have in the car, she drives me every single day and today will be no exception.

Once I'm sitting in the front seat of her Ford Fairlane, I explain it all. Wearing her light brown dress and driving with both hands on the steering wheel, she nods in understanding until I get to the part where I say I joined the boycott. A sad look comes over her face.

"Oh, Rabbit," she says. "Not baseball, too."

Silence descends on the car.

"I mean, basketball was one thing," she says. "But you're so good at baseball. It's such a sacrifice. You might have finished the season a hero like you did on the football team, running back kicks for touchdowns and throwing that option pass to Charlie. Now baseball is being taken from you, too. It doesn't seem fair."

For a few long seconds, I don't know how to respond. I feel the same sadness that she does. But I know, regardless of the outcome, that I did the right thing.

"There's lots of different ways to be a hero," I say.

She turns and stares at me. I'm about to ask her to keep her eyes on the road, when she does just that while shaking her head.

"Where do you…how do you come up with these things?" she asks. "That's the kind of thing I should be saying to you, not the other way around."

I shrug. I don't know how or why things pop into my head. Maybe it's because now I'm reading a lot. Books and articles about the Civil Rights struggle. Even so, I still don't know where thoughts like "different ways to be a hero" come from. I didn't get that out of any book. At least none that I can remember. Lots of times, the *wrong* thing pops into my head and slips out of my mouth before I can stop it. That happens *all the time*. Or I say the right thing at the wrong time.

We ride in silence until Mom pulls the car into the driveway. She rests her hand on my thigh and squeezes it.

"I wish you didn't always have to make these difficult sacrifices," she says. "I wish, for once, things would go easy for you. But words cannot describe how proud I am of you."

It isn't the first time Mom has used those words, but I couldn't be hearing them at a better time. My eyes well with tears, and I bolt for the front door.

*

I have no homework—many of today's classes were spent discussing Dr. King—so I pull out today's newspapers, the *Boston Globe* and the *Daily Evening Item*, and read all the front page articles, most of them about Dr. King. A little more than half a year ago, I had no use for any part of the paper but the sports section and the funnies, but right now I don't care what's happening with the Celtics, even though they've got their rescheduled playoff game tomorrow with Wilt Chamberlain and the Philadelphia 76ers. I don't care about Bobby Orr and the Bruins. And I don't care about Major League Baseball's postponed season openers. None of that seems important right now.

Sitting on the front room sofa, leaning forward, with the paper resting on the coffee table in front of me, I read a quote from our senator, Edward Brooke, the only black senator in the country.

"The crime is unspeakable," he says. "The grief unbearable. The savage act of the assassin must not be allowed to overshadow the higher vision which Martin Luther King shared with all of us."

That feels right. As do so many others.

Until I get to one by Texas governor John B. Connelly.

"King contributed much to the chaos and turbulence in this country," Connelly said, "but he did not deserve this fate."

My head practically explodes. *Contributed much to the chaos and turbulence in this country?* Because he fought for racial justice? Because a black person should be treated the same as a white person? Should have the same opportunities as a white person?

How could someone as stupid as this Connelly jerk—or more likely, as flat-out evil as he is—be governor of such a major state? No wonder a segregationist like Alabama governor George Wallace is running for president.

Because white people support them! Racist white people—like my father until he suddenly saw the light—vote for them. And they win elections. That opinion is the *majority*!

I want to crumple the newspaper and throw it against the wall. I want to kick the crumpled ball. I want to burn it.

Even Connelly's grudging qualifier that Dr. King didn't deserve to be assassinated for his contributions of chaos and turbulence, makes me sick. Really? He didn't deserve to be assassinated? That's the best you can say about Dr. King?

I hadn't thought that Texas was as bad as Alabama and Mississippi, but perhaps I've been wrong. I wonder how many chapters of the Ku Klux Klan are in that huge state. I wonder if George Wallace will win it in the November presidential election. I decide to root against every Texas sports team for the rest of my life. Even the Dallas Cowboys.

*

Mom and I somberly watch the Walter Cronkite newscast and its coverage of Dr. King's funeral, a mule-drawn wagon carrying his casket from a private service at a Baptist church to the public, open-air service at Morehouse College. The brief excerpts of the eulogies move both Mom and me. Sitting on my left, she grabs my wrist and squeezes it. We're still sitting there on the sofa, the Cronkite newscast credits rolling on the screen, when Dad comes in the front door.

"Sorry I'm late," he says as he sets down his tan briefcase.

Mom looks at me, takes in a deep breath, and says, "Let's get this over with."

I describe for him the baseball team situation and my decision to join the boycott. His shoulders slump and a weary look comes over his face.

"I don't get it," he says, shaking his head with a look of confused exasperation on his face. "The Negro kids—the black kids"—he corrects himself—"were going to make their point perfectly clear without your help. They didn't need you to join in. You knew that you were on thin ice with the coach. Yet…yet you felt obligated to pick a fight with him anyway."

I hold my tongue.

"You expect me to take off work because these games are so important to you," he says, "and I try. I really try. It's hard for a man in my position, but I try. A couple times I've been this close." He holds up his right hand with his thumb and forefinger a microscopic distance apart.

"You make me feel like a bad parent for not being there. I can see it in your eyes. But then…then you do something like this. Sabotaging yourself again. Just like with the basketball team."

He spreads his hands in a gesture of befuddlement.

"I love you, Rabbit, I really do," he says. "But why do you have to pick a fight every single time? Why do you have to make things so hard for yourself? Why not just once…let it go?"

# CHAPTER 13

I walk out to the fields behind the school, wearing a gray sweatshirt, gray sweatpants, and LEHS cap on my head. I'm surrounded by ten or so of my teammates, our cleats clicking on the parking lot asphalt between the school and the fields, but I feel very much alone. Charlie suggested that those of us involved in the boycott filter out separately to avoid the look of an us versus them division with our other teammates, and perhaps appear less threatening to Coach Kowalski. So he, Jessie, and J.P. Clayton are still back in the locker room while on my left, Moose Mahoney compares me graphically to a dog turd and on my right, a friend of his snickers.

That's okay. The day I care what a moron like Moose Mahoney thinks about me is the day I should get my head examined. What I do care about is what Coach Kowalski thinks, and also, I suppose, Coach Gilhooly. That has my heart in my throat and my mouth dry.

No one has stopped me and told me to turn in my uniform for failing to play yesterday. At least not yet. But the gauntlet of four coaches ahead of me at the metal backstop awaits, including Coach Kowalski, who may have decided he'll get more satisfaction by kicking me off the team publicly. A part of me wants to walk past them—if I'm allowed to get past them—with my head held high, proud of the stand I took. But this isn't the time to be strutting like a peacock, rubbing Kowalski's nose in what he no doubt views as my defiance.

So as soon as my cleats leave the asphalt and touch grass, I begin to trot toward the freshman field, my eyes focused on the ground before me, the patches of grass mixed with bare spots of dark brown dirt. I won't look to the assembled coaches thirty feet to my left unless they force me. I hold my breath as I pass them, feeling like a prisoner trying to sneak past the prison guards. I get a few feet past when Kowalski stops me.

"What do we have here?" he says.

I slow down, but keep going, hoping that Kowalski is just going to mock me in front of the other coaches. But he has more than that in store for me.

"Labelle, get over here!" Kowalski snaps.

I stop dead in my tracks and turn to face him. He's wearing his usual gray-with-maroon-letters LEHS warm-up suit and cap. The other three coaches, similarly attired, are arrayed behind him. He glares at me like I'm not worthy to live. I walk slowly in his direction, diagonally back toward the school, with all the dread of a man facing a firing squad. I can barely swallow. An involuntary shiver runs through me, and not because of the early-April gusts of cold wind.

"Yes, sir," I manage to say.

Kowalski folds his arms across his chest, resting them on his sizeable paunch. He spits a stream of brown tobacco juice in my general direction, though it falls several feet short.

"You think you can just show up when you choose?" he asks, his bushy gray eyebrows raised.

There isn't a satisfactory answer I can give to this question, either yes or no, and he knows it. I stare at him blankly. My ears burn as Moose and a few other players pass on my left, slowing down to gawk like drivers on the highway when there's an accident on the other side. More of the team spills out of the gym exit and across the parking lot.

"Answer me!" Kowalski snaps.

Even a dope like me knows I can't say that I can show up whenever I choose. So even though I know what's coming next, I say, "No, sir."

"No sir, you won't answer me?"

"No, sir," I say, my sense of dread deepening. "I mean I can't just show up when I choose."

"Really, now?" Kowalski scratches his chin in mock confusion. "Isn't that *exactly* what you did yesterday?" When I don't answer, he thunders, "*On the day your team needed you the most?*"

I open my mouth to respond, but no words come out.

"You abandoned your team in a moment of crisis!" Kowalski hollers. He turns from me to look at everyone frozen around us.

"Gather round!" he yells. "Down on one knee!" He tells Coach Gilhooly to fetch the three players already out on the distant freshman field, and we wait for the rest of the team to filter out.

It feels like an eternity, each second dragging out to feel like an hour. Surely, this is how the final moments of someone facing a firing squad feels. Kowalski is kicking me off the team. Of that there can be no doubt. He just wants to do it in front of everyone to maximize the impact, not to mention my humiliation and his satisfaction.

I immediately think of Charlie, Jessie, and J.P. Clayton, the three black players who attended school yesterday but chose not to play. Also Hector Martinez and José Fernandez. Are they also facing the same fate?

Slowly, the cleats of others click across the asphalt, and the muffled conversations fall silent as the players near our semicircle and see Kowalski glaring, his fury there on full display. I watch Charlie emerge from the gym exit and a little after him, Jessie.

It feels like they're getting here in slow motion. Like I might be seventy years old by the time they get here.

I want to warn them, give them some kind of signal, but what can I say or do? Besides, they're both smart. Smarter than me in almost every way. One look at Kowalski will tell them all they need to know.

When Charlie gets close, I look him in the eye and he gives a slight nod. He takes a position opposite me in the semicircle, his back to the school, presumably so we can look at each other without it being obvious.

"We have a situation here," Kowalski begins when all forty team members have gathered around him. The other three coaches stand arrayed behind him, their backs against the twenty-foot-high metal backstop. "It's a situation I addressed at the very beginning of this season with the freshmen." His eyes slowly scan the team from right to left, stopping on me. "I made it clear that this would not be a racially divided team. We would not repeat the mistakes of the basketball season."

Kowalski breathes in noisily through his nose.

"Now I understand that yesterday was a special day for the Negroes on this team," he continues. "It was a sad day for you. Many of you stayed at home, as the mayor said was your privilege. I can appreciate that even if I don't totally understand what you thought you were accomplishing by skipping school.

"Others, however, did attend yesterday, and I expected them to play baseball. It did not even occur to me that anyone who was here would refuse to play. We had important games for all three teams against Medford.

"But a number of you did refuse, and as a result, our freshmen team forfeited and our JV team almost had to forfeit as well because we nearly couldn't field that team either. Our varsity lost, 15–4, because it was without several of its best players, including our top two pitchers, and didn't have several of the top JV players to add as substitutes. *We got humiliated!*"

Kowalski shakes his head. He lets his words sink in as his glare goes from me on his left, then to his right, and then back again.

"I'm disappointed in all of you who failed to live up to your commitment to this team. You abandoned the team when it needed you the most. I do not understand how it was acceptable to come to classes, but not to play baseball.

"But I'm white, and I can't pretend to know what yesterday was like for those of you who are not. And I won't divide this team racially by meting out punishment along lines that would inevitably be almost one-hundred-percent racial."

Kowalski turns to me.

"There is only one individual here who has absolutely no excuse for yesterday's abandonment of this team," he says, his voice and eyes cold and hard. "And that's Labelle from the freshmen team. He's every bit as white as I am, so he has no excuse."

All eyes turn to me. My heart sinks.

"I suppose since he's just a freshman, I shouldn't care," Kowalski says, "but you all heard him on this very field talk back to me on the first day of practice. He had the audacity to challenge my authority and say that his commitment to this team was conditional on my not using certain offensive words or treating the Negroes on this team unfairly. As if he runs this team and not me."

Kowalski's eyes burn holes in me.

"I should have cut you then and there, for sassing me like that," he says to me. "But I didn't, God knows why.

"Well, I've lived up to my end of the bargain, as I always do," he says, his eyes now turning away from me to scan the entire team. "But Labelle here did not. He walked out on this team even though I have never used a racial epithet on a single player, and I never will. Even though I have treated every Negro on this team with complete fairness."

My mind screams of things to say, that this is totally unfair, that no one could have foreseen these circumstances, that Dr. King's death wasn't just a loss to the black community, it was a loss to us all, but a baseball-sized lump is lodged in my throat. I can't speak. I can't even swallow.

"As a result, Labelle is suspended from this team for one week, starting immediately," Kowalski says. "It should be for the entire season, but because I am a more than fair man, I am limiting it to just one week. He's to go back into the locker room and each day while we practice and play our games, he's to sit there and think about his commitment to this team. He isn't to do schoolwork or read books or anything. Just sit there and think about this team. Which I don't think he was doing yesterday at all. If he serves out this punishment, he will be allowed back on the freshmen team."

I feel as if Kowalski has just punched me in the gut, but I also feel at least some sense of relief. I'd been convinced he was going to kick me off the team forever, and if he was going to do it to me, he'd probably do it to Charlie, Jessie, and all the rest of them.

So it could be worse. It'll be a *looong* week. And pure misery to sit there in the locker room with nothing to do. But at least I'm still on the team.

My eyes widen as Charlie stands up. "Coach, this isn't right."

Jessie stands up, and then J.P. Clayton.

"No!" I say, my heart now aflutter in panic. This isn't a sacrifice I want them to make. "Don't do this, guys. Please." My eyes go from Charlie to Jessie to all the black players, not just Ray and J.P., but the ones looking back and forth at each other, not sure what to do. "It's just a week. Let's not make this any worse. Just a week. I'll do it."

I turn to Kowalski, whose lips are pursed, and eyes even colder than before.

"Coach, don't hold this against them," I say. "They're just being loyal friends. Don't take this personal. I'll serve the week, and then I'll be back working harder than ever. You just wait and see. I promise."

"Your promises don't mean much, Labelle," Kowalski says. He looks to Charlie, Jessie, and the others who are standing and says, "Back down on one knee and I'll try to forget this ever happened!"

With all the fervor I can muster, I motion with my hands for my friends to get back down. I silently mouth the words, "Please!" and "One week!"

Charlie's eyes lock onto mine. He doesn't want to go back down to one knee. But he's got to.

*Please!*

Finally, resigned, he does, as do all the others, though they sure doesn't look happy about it.

Kowalski nods in satisfaction. "Okay, let's play some baseball."

I'm so happy I convinced Charlie and the others to spare themselves and not pointlessly join me in misery, I almost turn to race out to the freshman field.

Then it hits me. Everyone else can head to their designated field, but not me. A bitter taste fills my mouth.

"Get moving, Labelle," Kowalski says. "And thank your lucky stars I'm a reasonable man."

It's a long, sad walk back to the locker room.

But nothing compared to the longest baseball practice ever.

*

Back in the locker room, I sit in the middle of one of the long wooden benches that separates two rows of gray metal lockers. There are a dozen rows of these lockers, each with about thirty of them facing out one way and another thirty on the backside of them facing the other. I'm in a middle row, about halfway down, staring at my locker.

This place used to be my friend, as comfortable as home. Really my second home. During the football season, the team captains got a stereo system to blast the Rolling Stones to get us jacked up for every practice and game. Mick Jagger singing "I Can't Get No (Satisfaction)" had me ready to run through a brick wall. Whether it was football, basketball, or baseball, this is where guys laughed and joked and got ready for the most fun part of their day, then came back sweaty and exhausted—though not so much with baseball—happy with their effort if not always the results.

Camaraderie. That's what this place was all about.

But now, it's as silent as a tomb. I'm the only one here, so if I so much as cluck my tongue it seems to echo off the walls. I've always, in a strange way, loved the awful smell of the locker room. The stench of sweaty bodies, uniforms drenched in sweat, unwashed jerseys and equipment. Sometimes, the Lysol that the janitors use to wash and disinfect the floors.

The odor is awful but wonderful, because this is home. Familiar and comfortable. An integral part of what I love to do most.

But now that I've been exiled here, the smell makes me nauseated, its tendrils creeping up my nose, planting themselves in my brain, making me convinced I'll have to endure this smell for the rest of my life.

I look at the clock on the wall over by the entrance to the gymnasium. It ticks softly.

*Tick, tick, tick.*

I've been here for less than five minutes. It feels like five years.

*Tick, tick, tick.*

This must be what solitary confinement is like in prison. In fact, I very much am in prison—baseball prison—and if this isn't solitary confinement, then I don't know what is.

*Tick, tick, tick.*

I'm going to go out of my mind.

# CHAPTER 14

The next day, it's every bit as bad. Even worse.

Before it starts, Moose Mahoney makes sure he finds me walking on the way to the locker room, three textbooks by my side, glumly anticipating my next few hours in solitary confinement. More than twice my size, he lumbers up next to me and, as other students bustle through the corridor, laughing and talking on their way home, he starts in with the taunts.

"Great practice there yesterday, Rabbit!" he says. And then, "What a great play you made, diving on that ground ball up the middle!" And then, "You were crushing the ball in BP!"

This, from a guy I considered a friend just a few months ago. Who carried me on his shoulders when I scored a couple big touchdowns. I guess you find out who your real friends are when times get tough, not when you're everyone's hero.

I ignore him until he calls me a Negro-loving fool, only he uses the other N word for Negro. I can't ignore that.

"Moose, I'm hating this suspension more than your pea-sized brain could ever imagine," I say. "But six days from now, I'll be back on the team and you'll still be an imbecile."

He blinks, momentarily stunned, then forces an awkward grin. The typical bully who can dish it out, but can't take it. And since his pea-sized brain can't come up with anything else, he repeats his more racist form of "Negro-loving fool."

I stop, hoping he'll just continue on without me, but he stops, too, a victorious look coming over his face. He's won and he knows it. My stopping to get away from him has shown him he's gotten under my skin.

Three guys behind us almost crash into us as Moose and I stand there, glaring at each other. One of them mutters, "What are you two clowns doing?" but they move on past us, glancing back over their shoulders and shaking their heads.

"Why are you doing this?" I ask Moose.

"Because I like it," he says, grinning, his face actually glowing with his victory. "And there's nothing you can do to stop me."

I shake my head in disgust, and resume walking toward the gym. Moose falls right in step alongside me. He launches into more taunts. "How many hits do you think you'll get in tomorrow's game?"

If I walk, he walks. If I stop, he stops. There's only one way to get rid of him.

Cradling my textbooks in my arm like a football, I sprint all the way to the gym.

*

Charlie and Jessie sit on both sides of me on the wooden bench between the two rows of lockers, their baseball caps sitting comfortably atop their modest Afros, their gloves and cleats at their sides. They're ready to head out to the field, but are keeping me company for an extra minute or two. I appreciate the gesture, but they really need to get going.

"Don't be late 'cause of me," I say.

"Don't worry, Cinderella," Charlie says with a grin. "It ain't midnight yet."

A couple minutes earlier, a couple of the other black players stopped by to also chat and lend a bit of support, but Charlie suggested they head out. The last thing Kowalski needs to see is most of the black players huddled around me. He'll be sure a conspiracy is underway.

"Just don't be the last ones getting out there," I say. "The whole point of me doing this is to minimize the damage. Make it so you guys ain't affected at all."

"I still say you should have let us walk off the field with you," Charlie says. Jessie murmurs his assent, and Charlie continues. "Can't believe you got me to get back down after I stood up. Ain't right that you take all of Kowalski's penalty yourself."

"That's right," Jessie says.

"No need for me to take you all down with me," I say. "A few more days and this'll all be over. If there's another battle, we'll fight it all together. I promise. But until then, let's avoid a war with Kowalski we can't win."

Charlie shrugs, unconvinced, but grabs his glove and whacks me playfully on the arm with it. Jessie does, too. They grab their cleats, which they'll put on just outside the exit, and they head out.

And my solitary confinement begins again.

*

I sit on the bench, staring at the lockers, wearing my practice jersey, sweatpants, cap, and cleats.

All dressed up but no place to go.

If only I could open my textbooks and do my homework. Or take out a sheet of paper and write Anna a letter. Or read a book. Or crouch at the end of the rows of gray metal lockers, and practice taking a lead off first base, then timing my jump just as the pitcher commits to throwing home and accelerating into full speed in three quick, short strides. Or drop onto the floor and do pushups, then pop up and do jumping jacks. Or do sit-ups. Or stretches. Or listen to the radio or my cassette tape of Anna's latest concert. Or watch TV.

*Something! Anything!*

But Kowalski is a cunning and vicious sadist. I'm not allowed to do *anything,* and if I'm caught, that's it. He'll get what he wants, which is me off the team.

Well, he isn't going to get it. I haven't seen any spies checking up on me, or any hidden cameras. But I'm taking no chances. I'm sticking to the letter of the law.

I'm…not…doing…*anything.*

I just sit there on my designated pinewood bench and stare at my gray metal locker. And think.

I wonder how many prisoners in solitary confinement have masterminded their best and most evil plans while just trying to stave off the boredom of doing nothing. Just trying to stay sane as the seconds drag on and on and on.

*Tick…*

*tick…*

*tick.*

Not that my thoughts are running to robbing banks or anything like that. But if you put a criminal in my shoes, what horrible possibilities would he consider? What heists or murders would he plot? Just because…he's got to think of something.

For me, only twelve minutes and thirty-nine seconds have gone by, and already I'm jumping out of my ever-loving skin.

I think of a poem to write for Anna. But I need to be able to write it down, not just so I don't forget the words, but also so I can *see* it. It doesn't make sense when it's only up in my head.

I'm going in circles.

*Tick…*

*tick…*

*tick.*

So I think about the essay assignment I have in English, but I'd really already figured out not only what I was going to write about but the opening lines, too. Without a pen and paper, there's not really much more to do.

*Tick…*

*tick…*

*tick.*

So I try to memorize definitions and dates for World History. But without looking at my textbook, I'm just repeating what I already know—the French Protestants were called Huguenots, Marie Antoinette lost her head in 1793, and Napoleon lost the Battle of Waterloo in 1815—and I'm missing out on what I don't know.

*Tick…*

*tick…*

*tick.*

Next thing you know, I'm conjugating French verbs in my head. *Attendre, attendant, attendu.* And after that, doing algebra word problems, like if a train traveling east 60 miles an hour approaches one traveling west at 45 miles an hour, how long before they meet if they start a hundred miles apart?

*Tick…*

*tick…*

*tick.*

You know you're going crazy when, just to pass the time, you're conjugating French verbs and doing algebra word problems in your head.

*

And so it goes. Each day, pure agony.

If I'm not trying to do homework in my head, I'm wondering if the Celtics can come back from their 3–1 deficit against Wilt the Stilt and the Philadelphia 76ers. (I decide they can because they're the Celtics even though it's never been done before in the NBA.) Or I wonder if the FBI is ever going to catch Dr. King's assassin. (They have to eventually, don't they?) Or I'm asking why it took the cities to burn in the wake of that assassination to get Congress to pass the Civil Rights Act. (Probably because there are too many politicians who think like George Wallace and that jerk from Texas, John Connelly. They aren't interested in equality.)

All the questions have terribly short answers. Nothing to occupy my mind for so much as a single minute.

Game days are the worst, I suppose, because those are usually the most fun, and suffering bitter losses to Lynnfield on Friday and then Revere the following Tuesday adds an extra layer of pain. But Saturday practice is no piece of cake either. Going to school for no other purpose than to sit and stare at the lockers for several hours, trying desperately not to go loco crazy, is its own kind of stab to the heart.

Each night on the phone, Anna tries to cheer me up, and tells me it will be worth it in the end. I will have stood up for my principles, and I'll be back on the team.

"Besides, you've always been a little crazy anyways," she says one time, and we both explode in laughter.

My father gives me "hang in there" encouragements and a slap on the back or squeeze of the shoulder, but I'm sure he thinks I should have just played the game and stayed out of trouble. Mom thinks, to use her phrase, that it's cruel and unusual punishment. She wants to complain at the next school committee meeting. Fortunately, I convince her to, in another one of her phrases, "let sleeping dogs lie," even though she isn't happy about it.

Charlie, however, seems to get angrier each day—angry *for* me, not *at* me—and remains upset that I convinced him and the other guys to back down and let me "take the whipping for all of us." He seethes as he, Jessie, and I sit on that pine bench between the lockers before they head out onto the field. I try to guide the conversation elsewhere, from the Celtics to the Red Sox to Motown music. But the only thing that takes even the slightest edge off that anger of his is the reminder that I only have a few more days left in my sentence.

"Man, you are the blackest white guy I ever met," he says, shaking his head.

I blink, stunned and speechless for a few seconds. His words touch my heart. They render silent all the vile words I've heard from Moose and, sad to say, a few others.

All that venom, gone. Powerless. As if the words had never even been uttered.

"Thank you!" I say.

Charlie's words help me make it through the last few days of my sentence, seven days that feel like seven years.

Then, unbelievably, I find out that the sentence isn't over after all.

# CHAPTER 15

My first practice back after my exile, I don't walk out to the freshman field. I don't jog. As soon as my cleats touch grass, I'm sprinting. My legs and arms are pumping, and I'm flying. Past the teammates around me. Past the coaches who either look amused or disgusted or befuddled—I can't tell which because they're only a blur off to my left, huddled at the backstop. Past the two players who somehow got out here before me.

Faster. Faster! *Faster!*

I gasp for breath when I reach the freshmen field's crabgrass-infested excuse for an infield.

That beautiful crabgrass-infested infield.

Never has crabgrass looked so good. I want to fall down on my knees and kiss the ground, but I belatedly realize I've made a spectacle of myself, and I probably ought to act like this isn't the first time I've ever stepped onto a field.

But it's great to be back. Even the chilly wind feels great on my face and bare arms.

The next day, Thursday, I feel every bit as euphoric. I've been set free. I'm back!

I'm like a boxer who never sees the roundhouse hook on its way to knock him out cold.

*

Friday arrives, and it's game time. I can't remember a baseball game I've waited for with more eager anticipation. All those hours spent sitting in the locker room, staring at the gray lockers and going out of my mind with boredom, will finally be worth it.

And adding icing to the cake, Anna will be coming to watch me play! She almost always has practice for band or for her chamber orchestra or the small jazz band she's part of. But for once, she can come watch me play.

"It's about time, man," Charlie says to me as he, Jessie, and I step onto the field together. The freshly cut grass smells sweeter than ever before, and my gray uniform with Lynn English stitched across the chest feeling like a prized possession. Charlie adds, "You paid dues that weren't yours to pay. But they paid."

He and Jessie will be with the rest of the JVs on the field to the right, while I'm on the left with the rest of the freshmen team, the twenty-foot-high metal fence dividing the two fields down our first base foul area and theirs on the third base side. The varsity, of course, is playing half a mile away at Fraser Field. I've set aside the galling fact that I really should be playing with Charlie and Jessie on the JVs. Today, I'm just happy to be playing.

"Knock 'em dead, guys," I say. We slap gloves, and I veer off to the left.

I see Anna and my mom talking, standing behind the backstop ten feet from where I'll step into the batter's box to lead off the bottom of the first inning. Anna is wearing a light blue jacket over her yellow dress. The wind blows her shoulder-length blond hair. I give a self-conscious wave of my glove, and my heart beats a little faster when she waves back and smiles.

I love that smile.

The team does its usual warm-up. The ball jumps off my bat with loud *cracks* when I get my swings in, then I do my best to get my uniform dirty before the game even starts, diving for infield grounders while others are at bat. I hold my glove to my face and drink in the sweet leather smell of a well-oiled glove.

It's great to be back. I've missed this so much. Finally, Coach Gilhooly summons us together around him, and reads off the lineup.

I'm not in it.

At first, I'm sure I've missed something. I've always batted leadoff, so I expected my name to get read first. But then I listen to see if I've been moved down to the middle of the order. Knock runs in instead of score them. That's okay with me.

But I'm nowhere to be found in the lineup!

"Coach?" I ask in bewilderment. Perhaps he's forgotten that I'm off suspension, that I'm back, ready to play.

Coach Gilhooly pretends he doesn't hear me, and when I persist, he looks past me, unable to look me in the eye.

My heart sinks. I feel all the air go out of me.

I've paid my dues, like Charlie said, and even kept the team from splintering apart. I'm not the egotistical type, but there's no question that I'm the best player on the freshmen team. I've been hitting close to a thousand, stealing every single base I've tried, scoring most of the team's runs, and fielding shortstop flawlessly.

*Now I'm not even in the lineup?*

Even Moose is looking at Coach Gilhooly like he's got three heads.

"Take a seat on the bench, Labelle," Gilhooly says, looking off into left field, a pained look on his face.

Punched in the gut again. Coach Gilhooly is just following orders. Kowalski's orders.

I'm still serving a sentence. Kowalski has tossed me in jail and thrown away the key.

*

My ears burn as I think of Anna here to watch me play, and all I'm doing is sitting on the bench. My humiliation at Kowalski's hands is now complete. It reminds me of a book I read about a prisoner of war who was tortured day after day as his captors tried to break his spirit.

Well, I think Kowalski has finally broken mine. I feel like I can barely breathe.

Eventually, every other player gets into the game, another self-inflicted loss. It's how Gilhooly tries to run the team. It won't be how it is on the varsity, he has warned us, but on the freshmen team everyone gets at least an inning or two.

Except me.

I'm the only one who never leaves the bench.

Kowalski has snapped me in two like a little twig.

*

I'd probably bawl like a baby all the ride home with my mom if not for one thing. Anna is riding with us, sitting in the back seat with me, and I can't be acting like a baby in front of her. Even so, I still have that sensation of having been sucker punched in the gut. I can barely breathe.

I'm not sure I even want to.

I've never felt this low in my life. Never felt so utterly betrayed. I've been angry and upset at things, of course. It seems like I've spent a lot of the last half year or so angry and upset. Trouble has followed me around, or as people like Coach Kowalski seem to think, I've chased after it.

But this is different. Worse somehow.

Coach Kowalski and I had a deal. I'd serve out his sadistic punishment. I'd sit there day after mind-numbing day, staring at the locker in front of me, inventing mental gymnastics of conjugating French verbs and doing algebra word problems and reciting the definitions of the stupid Huguenots to avoid going out of my mind with boredom. And after I paid my penalty—for what offense? for standing up for what I believed in?—I'd be allowed back onto the team.

I guess I made a deal with the Devil. Kowalski never actually promised that I would *play*. So he hasn't totally reneged on his promise. Not technically. But it's a total and complete betrayal

in every other way. Who would endure Kowalski's sadistic punishment only to then have to sit on the bench? Especially if he's
clearly the best player on the team?

And of course, the extra layer of humiliation is that Anna was
finally able to come watch me play, and she saw every other player
get into the game—even guys who can't play a lick—while I lan-
guished on the bench.

I'm just sick to my stomach over it all.

"I'm quitting the team," I say to both her and Mom. "I can't
take any more of Kowalski's torture. I just can't. What's the point?"

"I don't understand it," Mom says. "I was going to say something to the coach after the game. Give him a piece of my mind.
Really let him have it. But I wanted to talk to you first. I didn't
want to cause you trouble or say something that would make
things worse."

"How could things possibly get any worse?" I say bitterly.

"I'm sorry, Rabbit," Anna says. She reaches out and touches the
back of my hand. Somehow that makes me feel a tiny bit better,
though it does nothing to extinguish the fire of anger, humiliation,
and betrayal burning inside me. "It isn't fair. You don't deserve
this. You don't deserve any of it."

I nod glumly. I take her hand in mind. She gives it a squeeze
and smiles sadly at me.

I try to smile back, but I can't.

*

Charlie calls that night. I've already eaten dinner and talked to
Anna on the phone, so I'm upstairs in my bedroom, sitting at my
desk, trying to do homework while my brain refuses to cooperate.
I read the same sentence over and over, but all I can think about is
sitting on that cold, hard bench while everyone else played.

While Anna watched my humiliation.

And my anger grows and grows. My brain just wants to
explode. The quadratic equations I'm supposed to be solving for

algebra might as well be Einstein's Theory of Relativity. Coach Kowalski's ugly mug with its smug satisfaction and sadistic grin plastered all over it stare back at me from my textbook's pages, his crossed arms resting atop his beer belly. Spitting tobacco juice in my direction. I've actually had to take a new yellow No. 2 pencil out of my drawer and sharpen it because I gripped the previous one so hard it snapped.

Then I get the call from Mom at the foot of the stairs. "Rabbit, it's Charlie on the phone."

I dash downstairs, relieved to escape my pointless attempts at studying and also eager to talk to Charlie. Even though I consider him my best friend, we don't talk on the phone. He's never called me before, and I only called him when I heard of Dr. King's assassination. So I'm sure this is big.

"Hey, man, what's up?" I ask, and duck inside my father's empty office, pulling the extended, curly black cord around the corner and closing the door. I slide down to the floor, my back against the doorjamb.

"Heard what happened to you today," he says. "Didn't realize at the time 'cause we were playing, and that's what I was paying attention to, you know? Never thought to look over at your field and make sure you were playing. Why wouldn't you be?"

"Yeah," I say glumly.

"Well, don't do nothing crazy tomorrow, least not until you talk to me after practice," he says. Tomorrow is Saturday, and I've thought about just not showing up, and then explaining exactly why—that I'm quitting—after school on Monday right before practice. I'll march into Kowalski's office and let him know just what I think about his failure to live up to our bargain. That I clearly made a deal with the Devil. Then I'll march right back outside to where Mom will be waiting in the car to take me home and away from the baseball team.

Forever.

But Charlie has certainly caught my attention.

"Why?" I ask, sitting up straighter.

"I'm gonna talk to Kowalski," Charlie says. "Reason with him first. Tell him the whole team is watching how he's treating you. That he needs to treat you fair. Then if he won't listen to reason, I'm gonna hit him with the sledgehammer. All the brothers are going to walk out."

"No! Don't do that!" I say, alarmed. Suddenly, every muscle in my body has tensed. This isn't at all what I want.

"Why not?" Charlie asks. "You got us—me especially—to back down and let you take the penalty all by yourself 'cause it would just be the one week. Then it would be over. Those were your exact words. But it ain't over."

I sit there, frozen, unable to speak because I know he's right.

"How's it over if you sitting on the bench?" Charlie asks. "You, of all people! You the star on that team! You shouldn't even be on it. You should be up playing with me and Jessie."

"Yeah, but—"

"No buts about it, man."

"I appreciate it, but—"

"Why you arguing with me?" Charlie demands, an edge in his voice. "There ain't no question about it."

"I just don't want you guys to have to ruin your season because of me."

"What, the white boy can make grand gestures for his black friends, but not the other way 'round? Sacrificing for others be something only white people do?" Charlie has gone from having an edge in his voice to full-out angry. "You don't think our hearts are as big as yours? You don't think we as loyal to our friends as you are to yours?"

"No! I don't think that at all!" I cry out, barely able to speak, barely able to breathe, aghast at what Charlie is saying. He might as well have clubbed me in the gut with a baseball bat. It's as though all the air has gone out of me. I'm gripping the phone so hard my hands are shaking. There's a baseball-sized lump in my throat.

Somehow, I force out the words, "I just—"

But I can't even think of what to say next. I know that none of those awful thoughts were in my head. *You don't think our hearts are as big as yours? You don't think we as loyal to our friends as you are to yours?* I'd never think that.

Never!

So why aren't I willing to have my black friends sacrifice for me the way I've sacrificed for them?

"It isn't like that," I say, desperately trying to unscramble my thoughts. "Not at all."

"Then explain it to me," Charlie says. "'Cause I got to say, you ain't making any sense. If I didn't know better, I'd say that maybe you do look at us different. Like I ain't your friend. I just your *black* friend. And there a difference."

"Charlie, you ain't my *black* friend. You my friend. You my *best* friend. And it ain't that your heart and your loyalty are anything less than mine. You ain't only just as good as me. You're better. I just…"

I desperately try to put into words the jumbled thoughts that I feel.

"I'm just not someone who likes people sacrificing anything for me," I say. "Not you or Jessie or Anna or my mom. And when my mom sacrifices for me, like when she stood up to my father, I feel bad."

I'm appalled that those words about Mom standing up to my father have slipped out. That's a secret I shouldn't be blurting out, and only escaped because of the panic bubbling inside me. I quickly try to move on.

"I don't understand how my brain works," I say. "Sometimes I think it's defective. I don't know. I just know that it's easier for me to sacrifice for someone else, white or black, than to have a someone do it for me."

Charlie is quiet for what feels like an eternity. I wrack my brain for something else to say, but something tells me to shut up and let him think about what I've said.

"Well," he finally says, breaking the awkward silence, "you just gonna have to get used to the other end of the sacrifice stick. If I can't talk sense into Kowalski, it's gonna be war. Me and the brothers are gonna stick up for you, like you stuck up for us during the basketball season. And like you stuck up for us sitting out a baseball game that should have never been played, and then taking the punishment all alone. And if you dare tell me to keep my mouth shut, I'm gonna take it personal."

I swallow hard.

"Charlie, you're the best," I say. "Thank you. I can't imagine a better friend."

# CHAPTER 16

I'm on pins and needles before Saturday's practice. I wait inside the locker room as long as I can, hoping Charlie will emerge with some signal as to how things have gone with Kowalski. The other black players, whose lockers are scattered about the room, are abnormally quiet, at least so far as I can tell, and seem almost as on edge as I feel. When they do head out to the field, they glance down my row of lockers and look inquisitively, as if I somehow know the outcome. I give the first couple of them an awkward wave, silently thanking them for their support, but after that provokes odd looks from the white players around me, I just give a raise of the eyebrows to let passing black players know that I don't know anything more than they do.

Eventually, I have to go outside, too, even though Charlie is still nowhere to be seen. The suspense is killing me. My baseball career here at Lynn English is presumably hanging in the balance, and the same may hold true of my black friends. Not just best friends like Charlie and Jessie, but others with whom I've only interacted with on sports teams, and don't really know all that well, especially the older ones on the varsity. At the very least, their season is dangling over the precipice of Charlie's talk with Kowalski.

It feels so uncomfortable to have others sacrificing for me. But my heart is touched by what they all are prepared to do. Less than a week after a white man has assassinated their prophet of hope, they are being asked to possibly make a heroic sacrifice of their own for a white boy some of them barely know. And a white boy on the freshmen team, no less.

I glance over my shoulder as I walk across the asphalt, my cleats clicking with every step, and then slowly cross the varsity and JV fields on my way to the freshmen field. I'm not sprinting today. Right now, I'm slower than Moose Mahoney. Getting there without some sign from Charlie means going through the whole practice not knowing how things went with Coach Kowalski. It means dying all practice.

But still no sign of Charlie.

Alarm bells go off in my head, blaring loud and red. This can only mean trouble. If there had been good news, he'd be out here by now. With a sinking feeling in my gut, I know what must have happened. Kowalski crossed his arms in that smug, self-satisfied, no-one-is-going-to-push-me-around look and he told Charlie that every last one of us troublemakers can leave.

He might have even added a few racial epithets just to rub Charlie's nose in it. Let him know who's boss.

I just know it. And it makes me sick to my stomach.

Here on the freshmen field, we start batting practice even though the varsity and JVs just keep warming up. I'm not one of the first hitters. I'm not at shortstop, my usual position. I'm not even in the infield.

I'm stuck in right field, the place you hide your worst player because that's where the least amount of action is. *Right field.* As if yesterday's humiliation wasn't bad enough. *Right flipping field!* I can't believe it.

I'd walk right off the field right now if I hadn't promised Charlie I wouldn't do anything until he has a chance to fix things. Until he talks to me about his conversation with Kowalski.

But can there be any doubt? *Right field?* Just go ahead and strip me of all my dignity.

I try to swallow the lump in my throat. My ears burn as I think of Moose Mahoney, crouched behind the plate in his catcher's gear, laughing at me. The only thing is…I'm so far away from him, way out here in Palookaville, that I can't even hear his laughter. I can't even hear his taunts. But even though my ears can't hear them, my face burns with humiliation because I can hear them anyway in my head.

I just wish Charlie would get out here so I can escape this dungeon of horrors. I can't take it anymore. I hate Coach Kowalski. I hate Coach Gilhooly, who I know hasn't been making these decisions to humiliate me, but still is allowing himself to be Kowalski's stooge. I hate Moose Mahoney.

I hate all of them.

Eventually, Charlie and Coach Kowalski emerge from the back of the school. My attention is so drawn to the two of them crossing the asphalt, I barely hear the crack of the bat, and only belatedly realize that the batter—I haven't even noticed who it is—has hit a shot headed into the gap to my right. Not that I have a reason to care anymore. I know I'm finished on this team.

But I race after it based on pure instinct. I pump my legs faster and faster until they're a blur, my feet barely touching the ground. In that instant, I forget all of my problems. My mind is focused only on making up for my late break and getting to the liner in time. It looks like it's going to be just out of my reach. But at the last instant, I dive high and across my body for it, stretching every muscle to its fullest and—

I catch it!

It's a snow cone, the white of the ball poking out of the upper webbing of my glove, barely in there. So it's going to tumble out when I crash to the ground unless—

I turn my body as I fall through the air, my glove over my head, and I open it just a fraction of an inch and for a fraction of a second. Gravity pulls the ball down snug into the glove's webbing and I squeeze hard as I crash onto the ground. The jarring impact rattles my teeth and every bone in my body, and I go *ooof!* as it almost knocks the wind out of me.

But I hold onto the ball.

I roll over several times until my body's momentum finally comes to a halt. I lay there for a moment, stunned, wondering if all my body parts are still attached. And then finally, still lying on the ground, I hold my glove victoriously aloft, the ball still in it.

I think of all the times in our backyard up in Maine when I'd be playing catch with my dad and I'd tell him to make me dive for it. Or diving stops I made in the infield in practices and games. Well, this tops them all. It's the best catch I've ever made.

I bounce back to my feet and even though I suddenly hurt all over my body, and it's only batting practice, I pretend there's a runner at third trying to score on a sacrifice fly. Who does he think he's running against! I rear back and fire a rocket of a throw to Moose, standing at home.

As my fingers let go of the ball, I suddenly realize that this great catch, the best of my life, may be the final act of mine for this team. The anger and the resentfulness and yes, the hate, surge back within me. I hope my throw conks Moose square in the catcher's mask. *Boink!* It won't hurt him, of course. Masks are built to withstand foul balls coming off a bat inches away. I don't want Moose to get hurt, but a *boink* on his empty noggin would feel nice.

No such thing happens, of course. He reaches up, catches the throw, and although I can tell he caught it right in the palm and it stings, there's no humiliating *boink* in the head.

"What a catch!" Coach Gilhooly cries out. "Who is that, Carl Yastrzemski out there?"

But then he realizes who he's praising. The pariah. Stunned, he recoils as if he's been slapped, then stares down at his clipboard as several of my teammates cheer.

It's only then that I notice Charlie running out to our field. And I know that my great catch has also been my final one for this team.

It's over.

*

If not for Charlie, this would feel like a firing squad. I'm standing with him and all four coaches behind the varsity field backstop, on the spectator side, as practices continue on the three fields. The gray metal backstop towers behind me as I face the coaches: Kowalski, centered a step in front of the others, his short and stocky assistant, Particelli, and Gilhooly behind on his left, and JV Coach Fitzgerald on the right. Charlie stands behind all of them, looking at me over Kowalski's right shoulder, his Afro poking out of his LEHS baseball cap. His glove covers what I'm starting to think is a huge grin. His eyes are filled with a joy I haven't seen in a long time.

Charlie must have won! He must have talked Kowalski out of my never-ending punishment, either through reason or threat of losing all the black players. Looking at Kowalski's stone face, I can't read which one, but this isn't a firing squad. It's an unlocking of my prison cell. It's got to be. But I can't let that hope show on my face. It might anger Kowalski and undermine whatever Charlie has achieved.

And to be honest, I don't dare believe it until I hear it with my own ears. Last time I thought I'd been set free, I found myself glued to the bench, humiliated in front of my girlfriend. So I stand here, my heart in my throat and my mouth dry as cotton. I nervously tap my gloved hand against the side of my leg.

Coach Kowalski gives me an appraising look. He nods almost imperceptibly, then puts his hands on hips. He takes a deep breath, his large chest expanding. He spits a stream of tobacco juice, and clears his throat. His eyes narrow.

"I've had a talk with Mr. Watson here," Kowalski says, giving a nod of the head to Charlie behind him. "He made a very persuasive argument on your behalf, Labelle. I've been concerned about you. You seem to be a ringleader of sorts when it comes to protests and that sort of thing. And you've certainly got a big mouth."

I swallow hard.

"I was convinced you were a troublemaker that this team would be better off without, despite your obvious talents," Kowalski continues. "I was rather hoping you'd quit this team and I'd be rid of you. Good riddance to bad rubbish. Much to my chagrin, you didn't."

Kowalski scratches the whisker stubble on his chin, as if he's deep in thought.

"Mr. Watkins, however, has convinced me that instead of you being a divisive force on this team, you've actually been one that has held the team together." Kowalski grits his teeth. "I still think you were wrong to refuse to play that game last week, and I'll never change my mind about that. I was very disappointed in that action, and hope to never see it again.

"But the next day when I sent you back to the locker room and gave you a one-week suspension as punishment, Watkins and others were ready to join you. They had also missed the game, and didn't think it was fair that you suffer the punishment, much less do so all by yourself. Watkins stood up, and I believe Jessie Stackhouse and others were beginning to as well.

"If a large number of our Negroes had walked off with you, that would have ripped this team apart. Apart across racial lines. Just like the basketball team. Watkins here"—Kowalski gives another nod toward Charlie—"pointed out that you weren't the rabble-rouser I had thought you were. If you were, you would have encouraged your friends to join you. Instead, you practically begged them to get back down on one knee and let you take the punishment yourself."

Kowalski gives Charlie a sour look.

"According to Watkins, you didn't divide the team; you held it together. You didn't inflame what was already a tense situation;

you tried to defuse it. You weren't the troublemaker you easily could have been; you were a peacemaker.

"Well, I'm not going to nominate you for the Nobel Peace Prize like Mr. Watkins here. I'm never going to like you, Labelle." Kowalski glowers at me as if to reinforce his point. "But at least some of what Watkins said about you seems to be true. You did stop the others from joining you. And I suppose that did hold the team together. You didn't even cause trouble, as I had expected you would, after the one-game benching I ordered Coach Gilhooly to give you."

Kowalski draws in a deep breath of air and exhales.

"As a result, I'm making the following probationary move conditional on your best behavior." He crosses his arms across his chest. "Based on your exceptional performance on the baseball field, and your surprising role as an apparent peacemaker, I'm elevating you to the junior varsity."

My jaw drops. My eyes bug out like a cartoon character. I feel almost lightheaded.

Did I actually hear that? Or did I hear what I wanted to hear? Kowalski must have actually said it because there's no way my imagination could have come up with this. I never saw this coming. I glance at Charlie, who has finally lowered his glove, exposing an ear-to-ear grin.

It's true!

I leap into the air, my hands thrust up to the sky in euphoric jubilation. I jump up and down a few more times as if I'm on a pogo stick.

*I'm on the JVs! I'm on the JVs!*

Kowalski's sour look, mirrored by his assistant, Particelli, reminds me of my manners. The other two coaches are only barely camouflaging their happiness, holding a hand to their mouth to conceal the grins I saw break out on their faces, but this couldn't have been easy for Kowalski. And my euphoria may easily be taken as me rubbing his nose in it.

"Thank you, Coach!" I say, composing myself. "Thank you! Thank you! Thank you!" I pound my fist in my glove. Suddenly, I notice all the best baseball smells. My well-oiled glove. The freshly cut grass. Even the stale sweat from my LEHS baseball cap.

"Thank you!" I say again, my mind in a blur and unable to come up with anything else.

"One problem out of you, Labelle," Kowalski says, "and I'll bust you back down to the freshmen team so fast you won't know what hit you. Or I'll just cut your troublemaking ass and be done with you for good." He spits on the ground with what seems like extra ferocity. "Don't think I won't do it. Just give me one reason and you're gone!"

I nod my understanding. "Yes, sir!"

"Now get going!" Kowalski growls. "Time's a-wasting."

I start to sprint back out to the freshman field, to Crabgrass Central, cutting around the backstop and down the varsity third base foul area. I'm past the twenty-foot high fence that separates the top two fields before I joyfully realize my error and veer left.

To the JV field.

Where I belong.

*

After practice, Charlie and I approach Mom's blue Ford Fairlane parked in the semicircle in front of the school. I open the passenger side front door, duck down, and shout, "I'm on JVs!"

Mom's eyes widen. "*What?*"

I repeat the astonishing news, grinning ear-to-ear.

She shakes her head in disbelief. "You're kidding!"

But I'm not kidding and Mom knows it. This is the last thing I'd kid about.

"But you didn't even play the last game," she says. "You got benched! What happened?"

Still standing outside the car, I point over my shoulder. "Charlie happened!"

Charlie grins and walks behind the car. He opens the driver's side back door. We usually give him a ride on Saturdays.

"Wait just a second!" Mom says. She springs out of the car and gives Charlie a big hug. "Thank you!" Then she races to my side and wraps her arms around me. She squeezes so hard she practically knocks the wind out of me. She smells of soap and talcum powder. Over and over, she says "I'm so happy for you! I'm so happy for you! I'm so happy for you!" Her body shakes with emotion.

Other times, I might be embarrassed at this show of emotion, especially with other members of the team streaming out of the school's front doors. But not today. Not even if stupid Moose Mahoney walks by and starts making fun of me.

Today, I'm bulletproof to all of that. Nothing can hurt me.

When Mom finally lets go and races back around to the other side and climbs in, I realize my cheeks are wet, and I'm not entirely sure they're her tears. I wipe them dry before I shut the front door and join Charlie in back.

"This calls for a celebration!" Mom says. "How about we go to Fauci's Pizza?"

Like that suggestion is *ever* going to get turned down.

"Sure," Charlie and I say in unison, grinning even a bit more broadly, if that's possible.

"I'll stop at the corner pay phone and call your mother so she doesn't get worried," Mom says to Charlie.

"You don't have to," he says. "She works until six tonight."

"Okay," Mom says. "What about Jessie? Would he like to join us?"

"He said he's got a spring league hockey game," Charlie says. "He's *always* got a hockey game to go to."

"Okay, but there's one other call I should make," Mom says. "Don't get your hopes up, Rabbit. It isn't to your father. He'll be delighted, of course, and I'll make a cake—a Boston cream pie with extra cream in the middle just how you like it—and we can celebrate when he gets home. But you know how he is about personal phone calls at work and getting out early. Even on a Saturday." She pulls to the curb and opens the door. "This will only take a second, then you'll have to tell me all about the wonderful news."

She pops into the little convenience store on the corner to make the call and is back out before I can pump much of anything out of Charlie, who hadn't wanted to talk about it inside school where the wrong people might overhear him.

"So tell me, Charlie, what on earth did you do?" Mom asks as we head down Chestnut Avenue for Fauci's. "I thought it was all over for Rabbit. I thought he was finished."

*So did I*, I think.

"Man, it wasn't easy," Charlie says. "Kowalski's one tough nut to crack. No matter what I said, he just sit there behind his desk in that tiny office of his, crossed his arms, and say back, 'Labelle had no excuse to skip that game. I knew he was a troublemaker from the moment I laid eyes on him. And he proved me right. A troublemaker with a capital T.'"

Mom gives a quick glance over the front seats at me, and gives me a look, her eyebrow raised.

"Thought I was gonna have to club him over the head with one of them Louisville Sluggers he keeps in the corner of his office," Charlie says.

For a fraction of a second, my mind flashes back to a few months ago when thugs attacked us with sawed-off bats during the basketball protests. My heart instantly jackhammers inside my chest until I push that image away.

"Kowalski just wouldn't listen," Charlie continues. "Problem was, I didn't think the threat of all us black players walking out would change his mind either. In fact, it would have backfired. I'm sure of it. That man is just too stubborn."

Mom gives a knowing nod.

"Well, I'd been talking as white as I could, you know? Not at all like a brother. But since that wasn't working, I tried…" Charlie shrugs, and a faraway look comes to his eyes, there and then quickly gone. "Since this was all about him, I tried to talk like I was Dr. King giving a speech. You know, like a black preacher with the, ah, the phrasing, the timing, they call it the cadence of a black church. You ain't never been to one, but you've heard the man."

I nod, trying to imagine Charlie sounding like Dr. King and having a tough time of it.

"I got what my momma calls righteous indignation in me, and I got preaching to Kowalski. Not shouting at him, but I was preaching. And he sure didn't like it. His eyes grew wide like he couldn't believe what he was hearing, and his face burned red like he was about to explode. But I was so angry, so full of my righteous indignation, I didn't *care* what he did to me. I didn't *care* if he threw me off the team.

"So I say, 'Rabbit Labelle didn't *tear* this team apart. He *held* it together! He wasn't no *troublemaker*. He was a *peacemaker*! When some of us *stood up* to support him, he told us to *sit down*. Why? So he could take the penalty alone. *Alone!* And why? For the good of the *team*!'

"I got going so good I finished by saying that just letting you play wasn't enough. He needed to *credit* you for what you done—for being the peacemaker—by putting you on the JV team where you belong. I tell you, I got him so convicted of his sin, he was squirming in his seat.

"I knew he either gonna treat you right or he throw me off the team. Nothing in the middle."

I'm so moved my eyes pool with tears. My heart is in my throat.

"Thank you, Charlie," Mom says from the front seat.

Unable to speak, I clench my fist and pound it on the seat between us.

*

And when I thought it couldn't get any better, it did. We find out why Mom made that phone call from the corner convenience store's pay phone. The three of us are sitting in a wooden booth at Fauci's, at the back of two rows of booths and tables, a red-and-white plaid tablecloth covering the table. We're waiting for our pizza, salivating at the smells of tomato sauce, garlic, melted cheese, and grilled steak for sub sandwiches that fill the air.

Then Anna walks in, wearing a peach-colored dress with a matching bow in her shoulder-length blond hair. She smiles shyly, then looks from me to Charlie to my mom and then back to me.

"My mom got a call that there was a celebration I'd want to be part of," Anna says. "So what's the good news?"

# CHAPTER 17

In my first few games on the JVs, Coach Fitzgerald—or Coach Fitz as he's called—moves me around the infield and outfield positions, probably to gauge where I can help the team the most, but maybe to also avoid the ruffled feathers that can occur when a new guy takes over someone's job. He also starts me hitting sixth in the lineup. Pretty soon, though, I'm leading off and I'm the regular shortstop, displacing Stevie Papadopoulos, who moves over to second base where Donnie Rankin had made errors in three games in a row and wasn't hitting either so he really couldn't complain.

It's great to be on the JVs, playing where I always knew I belonged, and especially fun to be playing with Charlie and Jessie. Except on the days when one of them pitches—they're two of our best on the mound—we make up three-quarters of the infield with Charlie at the hot corner—third base—and Jessie at first, where his height makes him a natural to be able to snag high throws. They also bat third and fourth in the order because they have a ton of power, so we also represent three of the top four spots in the lineup.

I'm proving I belong here, getting on base almost two out of every three times and stealing bases like Maury Wills with the Dodgers when he set the major league record a few years ago with 104 thefts while getting caught only 13 times. I'm getting one or two steals just about every game, taking my lead and reading the pitcher so I take off at just the right time. I haven't gotten thrown out yet.

"Way to set the table," Coach Fitz tells me after many games, referring to me getting on base and into scoring position where Charlie and Jessie can knock me in with their doubles, triples, and home runs. Coach Fitz is almost totally unlike Coach Kowalski, slim and fit, probably only thirty years old, with thick, dark brown hair parted on the side. Most of all, he's very supportive, although after Coach Kowalski finally relented and let me not only actually play in the games but do so on the JVs, I can't really complain about him anymore.

April turns to May and the cool air grows warm and then hot. We go on a winning streak, winning seven straight, including a big one over our cross-town rival, Lynn Classical, before dropping one to Swampscott, then win another five to close out the regular season. It's really as much fun as baseball gets, and I'm sure I appreciate it even more because it was so hard to get here.

The only negative is that Jessie will be leaving us after this year.

He, Charlie, and I are walking through the corridors on the way to the front entrance after practice, our footfalls echoing in the long hallways and our hair still wet from the showers, when Jessie drops the bomb. At least on me. Turns out, he told Charlie a couple days ago, which I guess makes sense since the two of them are much closer friends than he and I are.

"You can't say anything—it's a secret for now—but I got a full scholarship to play hockey at Springvale Prep," Jessie says. "It's a prep school in New Hampshire. They've won four straight New England championships, and that league is the toughest in the country. Three of their graduates played on the 1960 Olympic team that won the gold medal, and one is a star at Princeton and should play in the NHL after he graduates. That's my dream, to play in the NHL someday."

"Wow!" I say. "That sounds great. We'll miss you, of course." I grin. "Although I won't miss you crushing me on the football field."

Jessie grins back.

"It's a great school," he says. "Almost everyone there goes to schools like Harvard or Yale or Princeton after they graduate. I'm going to have to study my butt off."

"So you'll live there?" I ask, even though I know the answer.

I think of my own parents and how they would react to that idea. Before my father changed and we were still at war all the time, he probably would have loved to get rid of me. Make me someone else's problem. Hope they could make "a man out of you." But Mom would never let me go. And now, I'm not so sure Dad would be willing to let me go either, though maybe if the opportunity was as great as this Springvale Prep sounds. "Your parents are okay with that?"

Jessie's face clouds over.

"At first, they wouldn't let me go," he says. "Said it was too dangerous. But after Dr. King got shot and all the riots broke out, and then a rock got thrown through our front window and our house got spray-painted with that friendly message"—Jessie grimaces at the memory—"they decided there wasn't any place that was safe."

"Why would a prep school in New Hampshire be dangerous?" I ask, confused.

We get to the front entrance, but don't leave. Our rides can wait. Jessie motions us off to the side, forty feet to the right of the big bank of three double-doors, out of earshot of the other team members coming up behind us. They glance our way curiously, as if wondering what plot we're hatching, then push on a gold-colored metal bar on one of the doors, it clicks loudly, and they leave.

"I'm going to be the Jackie Robinson of that school," Jessie says "Springvale Prep has never admitted a black student. I'm the first. Me and another kid who's going to play basketball. We'll both play football, too. We're breaking the color line there."

My jaw drops and my eyes widen. I'm struck by the magnitude of the achievement.

"Wow!" I say, knowing I'm repeating myself, but unable to come up with anything more intelligent until I finally manage, "That's amazing!"

Jessie thanks me, spreads his broad shoulders, and flashes a proud, yet haunted, smile. "I'd like to think Dr. King would have been proud."

We all ponder that in silence for a few moments.

"I wish I could do something that impressive," I say.

Charlie shakes his head and gives me a look. "Be thankful you don't need to."

*

The team breezes through the limited playoffs allotted to JV teams until it hits a brick wall in the league championship game. In the quarterfinals, we defeat Revere, 7–2, with Charlie and Jessie both hitting monstrous inside-the-park home runs to knock me in after I get on base. Then in the semis, we rout Gloucester, 10–1. I hit two doubles, a single, and get a walk in my four at bats, and score all four times, twice on doubles by Charlie, and twice on two more home runs by Jessie.

We're an offensive juggernaut until we face Swampscott in the championship game. The Big Blue gave us our only defeat over the last thirteen games, and that was without their secret weapon, a tall, skinny pitcher named Keating who throws the most unhittable knuckleball this side of Hoyt Wilhelm and Phil Niekro. I can only guess at the reason he isn't on the varsity. Either the Swampscott varsity coach already has a couple Bob Gibsons in his rotation, or more likely, he doesn't trust the unpredictability of a knuckleballer, who can be unhittable one game and then not be able to throw a strike the next three.

Either way, Keating is pitching the game of his life against us in the biggest game of the year. It's a warm, cloudless sunny day, and it's a home game on the number one field in back of the school. By the second inning, the smell of the loose infield dirt is in my nostrils and my uniform is filthy dirty—just how I like it—from me diving to make stops, then popping up to throw the runner out at first base. Anna and my mom are seated in the wooden stands along the first base line, behind a chest-high, gray metal fence that runs all the way down the foul area. There are about thirty other spectators, all friends and family, about normal for JV games. The varsity team gets bigger crowds, playing at Fraser Field, but it got knocked out of the playoffs early. Its season is over.

Jessie is shutting down the opposing lineup, but so is Keating, the knuckleballer. His pitch comes in slow as molasses, not even spinning like a curveball, and you think you're going to pound it out of the park or at least into the outfield alley, but then it darts unpredictably away as if it has a mind of its own and it's intent on avoiding your bat. You look foolish whiffing on a pitch that seems like one your grandmother could pound. Then feeling frustrated, you swing even harder and spin yourself like a corkscrew halfway to China.

I've never seen anything like it. None of us can hit it. The catcher can't catch it. And the umpire is having a heck of a time calling balls and strikes. In fact, the umpire's toes keep getting hit with the pitch after the catcher misses it. His toes have more hits than our batters. Keating may be awful two out of every three games, walking the entire lineup, but he's on fire today, at just the right time for him and the wrong time for us.

Through seven innings, which is regulation length in high school, he's got a no-hitter going. He has walked five batters, but those have unfortunately been our slowest players who can't take advantage of the pitch's wild nature on the basepaths. In fact, three of them immediately got erased by double plays. We haven't gotten a single runner to second base. Keating is totally shutting us down. So we head into extra innings with the score still 0–0. Jessie gives way on the mound to Charlie—they're our top pitchers—but Keating stays on the hill for Swampscott.

Finally, I come up in the bottom of the ninth with the bases empty and one out. I've struck out twice and hit a feeble dribbler to first for an out in my other at bat. I've totally failed to set the table for Stevie Papadopoulos, who bats second, and then Charlie and Jessie.

Time to get the job done. I've *got* to get on base.

"Let's go, Rabbit!" Anna cheers. Her voice always makes me smile, but I have to tune it out and focus.

Just me and the knuckleballer. Just me and him.

"Let's go, Rabbit!" calls out another voice, an unexpected one.

Dad? He's finally come to one of my games?

*Dad!*

I step out of the batter's box to collect my thoughts. This is a far tougher voice to tune out. Of course, I used to tune my father out on a regular basis at home. It was a matter of survival when we were constantly at war with each other. But things are different now, and this is very much different. This isn't tuning out the old criticisms and accusations, and tuning out of all the old arguments.

This is tuning out a voice I've desperately longed to hear on this field. Now, for the first time in what feels like forever, I'm finally hearing it.

*Tune it out! Tune it out!*

"Let's go, Rabbit!" Dad calls out again.

"Sorry," I say to the umpire as I dab at my eyes with my shirt sleeve. "Dirt in my eye."

Which is a lie, although if I keep dabbing at them with my grit-covered sleeve, it'll become true soon enough.

*Tune it out,* I tell myself. *Tune it out! The game depends on you. Tune it out.*

Just me and the knuckleballer. Just me and him.

Just me and him.

The first pitch comes in at above eye level until at the last instant, too late for me to swing, it darts sharply down right over the plate.

"*Stee-rike!*" calls the umpire as the catcher, who whiffed on it, chases the ball to the backstop.

Patience, I tell myself. You've got this. Focus.

Just me and the knuckleballer. Just me and him.

The next two pitches are wild ones that almost hit me, one almost in the head and the other in the knee.

I foul off the next one. Two balls and two strikes.

Just me and the knuckleballer. Just me and him.

The pitch comes floating in so slowly it almost begs for me to crush it. "Hit me!" it seems to say. "Hit me all the way to Boston!"

But I have to stay in control. If I try to crush it, I'll corkscrew myself halfway to China and strike out.

So I wait patiently, and in control. Hands poised to slap it to right field.

I swing, eye on the ball, and…

…the ball drops off a cliff.

I miss it completely. Strike three. The wind goes out of my sails. Another strikeout! Another failure.

Until I realize the catcher scrambling to the backstop after the ball.

I take off for first base, accelerating quickly into top speed, my feet barely touching the ground, my legs a blur. A catcher must catch a third strike unless a runner is already at first base with less than two outs. So although I've struck out, I'm alive until the catcher throws me out at first.

And he isn't going to do it.

I fly down the base path. As I reach first base, I stretch out my lead leg and touch the base just before the throw cracks into the first baseman's mitt.

"Safe!" calls the first-base umpire, and draws his two hands across each other in the cutting motion that gives visual confirmation of that call.

*Yes! I'm alive!*

I only vaguely hear the cheering and clapping. Nothing is going to distract me now.

I know exactly what I'm going to do. Coach Fitz flashes the steal sign, tapping his gray LEHS cap twice, then his nose, and then his right arm, but I don't need any signal to tell me I've got to get into scoring position. We've done nothing against Keating all game. We need to generate a run on the basepaths. Only Coach Fitz giving the red light would stop me, and he's no dummy. He knows we need a stolen base right now.

However, so do Keating and his catcher. They know I'm going. Coach Fitz's steal sign may be secret, but he might as well yell out, "Run for your life, Rabbit!" because anyone who knows anything about baseball knows I'm going.

And there's nothing Keating and his catcher can do about it. They can't stop me. As the knuckleball floats lazily toward home, I'll be racing toward second. If the catcher actually finds the dancing knuckleball in his glove, it'll still be too late.

Second base is mine. It's as if I'm already there. Third base, too.

I take my lead off first, then easily get back when Keating throws over. Since he can't throw a knuckleball to the first baseman, who'd have a tough time catching it, he has to change his grip to a fastball grip before he throws it over. He might as well advertise he's throwing the ball to first.

So I take an even bigger lead until I see him change grips, then I'm already heading back before he throws it. I don't even have to dive.

He tries to trick me the next time, but I'm onto him. I notice that he isn't taking his usual knuckleball grip, something he telegraphs every time, but doesn't matter to the batter because knuckleballs are all he throws. You know it's coming. You just can't hit it.

But to a base stealer, the telegraphing means everything. It's why I watch all pitchers closely. These aren't major leaguers. They all have weaknesses. I just need to find them. So I only take a normal lead, and dive back safely when he throws over.

Again, Keating takes his fastball grip. This time, though, he throws to the plate, but not a meatball that Stevie Papadopoulos—short and wiry in his batting crouch—can hit hard. It's a pitchout, a throw off to the side, far out of the strike zone, unreachable by the batter, and up at chest level so the catcher is already out of his crouch and can throw out a base stealer. This was their only hope to get me, but I was onto them and haven't taken off. I'm still at first base. Coach Fitz's steal sign to me always comes with a qualifier. I can ignore it, if I think there's a pitchout.

Keating gives me a dirty look when he gets the ball back. He stares at me for a few seconds, obviously wondering how I knew he was pitching out, thinking I must have stolen the sign flashed by the catcher. He summons the catcher for a quick conference, shaking his head and looking over at me as they talk. The conference ends, the catcher goes back behind the plate, and Keating gets ready for his next pitch.

He telegraphs that it's a knuckleball, so I take my extra lead, and when he goes to the plate with the pitch, I'm off for second. Coach Fitz gave Stevie the take sign so he doesn't even swing at a ball that bounces in the dirt and past the catcher.

As I near second base, I glance over my shoulder at the plate. I see the ball hit the backstop at a funny angle and carom away from the catcher. So I make no slide, but instead roar hard around second, make a mad dash for third, and dive in safely headfirst.

I'm enveloped in a cloud of dust from the dirt my slide kicked up. I can taste the grit on my lips as I get up. I take only a second to brush dirt off my uniform as I stand on third base. I want to leave most of it on there. I like my uniform dirty.

"Way to go, Rabbit!" I hear from the stands and our team's dugout just in front of the stands. "Way to go!"

But I tune it out. No distractions.

I've got to get home. I've got to score.

I take the biggest possible lead off third. Keating stares at me. Daring me to try the most outrageous play in baseball, stealing home. The thought crosses my mind. It's almost always a bad gamble, and especially against a right-handed pitcher, who's staring directly at you. A lefty who can't see you taking off? Maybe. But with a righty, I'd have to count on the catcher bobbling the pitch or missing it entirely. Normally, a long shot.

But not with a knuckleballer. Keating's catcher has been boxing the ball all over the place. This might be our best shot. It would be worth trying with two outs and a weak hitter up, but there's still only one out and we're at the top of our lineup.

I glance at Coach Fitz, who seems to be reading my mind. He shakes his head no. Well, that settles it. I'll have to wait for a hit, a sacrifice fly, or the ball to get by the catcher.

With Stevie at the plate, the ball does elude the catcher twice, but each time, as I prepare to race home, I see it carom off the backstop directly to the catcher and have to race back to third.

Stevie strikes out, putting it all on Charlie's shoulders. Two outs in the bottom of the ninth. The score tied, 0–0. And Charlie's had no more luck with the knuckleball than I have. He's struck out all three times.

Got to score. Got to score.

Coach Fitz doesn't give me the sign to steal, but he doesn't put up the stop sign either. I'm on my own. He's trusting me to use my own judgment, something I really like about him.

On the first pitch to Charlie, I take off for home. But it's only a bluff. I stop immediately, slamming on the brakes. I'm not really stealing home, but Keating flinches and takes a flagrant hitch in his motion before he continues it and throws the knuckleball to the plate. It's a textbook balk, exactly what I was hoping for, as clear an example of a balk as possible, but the umpires miss it completely.

"That's a balk!" Coach Fitz yells. "*That's a balk! That's a balk!*"

He yells it over and over with increasing ferocity, and for good reason. That should be the game. After a balk, the pitch is dead and the runner advances.

I should have scored. We should have won the game. Instead, the home plate umpire simply called a strike on Charlie.

It's been a source of frustration for me all season. I've induced balks about a dozen times, but only gotten the call three times. Every other time, the umps either missed it or decided not to call it for some reason, perhaps thinking it inappropriate below the varsity level and especially inappropriate back when I was playing on the freshmen team.

But this is the JV league championship game! The title is at stake!

"How did you miss that?" Coach Fitz yells, his face red with rage. "It was as plain as the nose on your face! That was the winning run!"

The home plate umpire looks cluelessly from behind his mask at Coach Fitz, then at the first base ump, the only other umpire, who is turning red himself, only it's from embarrassment. He knows he blew the call, but it's too late now to change it.

We should have won! The blown call has taken the win away from us.

As the home plate ump motions toward Coach Fitz with his hands pressing downward—settle down!—and then finally tells him he'll throw him out if he doesn't stop, I tell myself to push away the frustration and forget it.

It's over. Nothing we can do about it now. Just have to score anyhow.

Eventually, things settle down. Keating throws over to keep me close—the third baseman keeps sneaking over—but I get back easily each time.

Got to score. Got to score.

Charlie takes the second pitch as a ball. The catcher boxes it around, so I take a few steps down the line, but he keeps the ball in front of him so I dash back to third.

He isn't as lucky the next time. Charlie takes a swing, but even as the knuckleball dips away from his bat, it also eludes the catcher, who gets the pinky finger edge of his glove on it before it bounds away down the first base line.

I race for home, still ready to slam on the brakes after two strides and get back to third if it looks like a bad gamble, but no, this is the best chance we'll get.

Do or die.

I pass the point of no return, and I'm flying. I will my feet to barely touch the ground. I drive my legs to piston faster and faster.

Keating rushes in from the pitcher's mound to cover home plate. Charlie backpedals out of the batter's box.

*Faster!* I tell myself. *Faster!*

Keating awaits me at home plate, but he doesn't have the ball. Not yet.

Out of the corner of my eye I see the catcher flip the ball toward him.

I dive, stretching my fingers for the plate.

I feel the home plate rubber slide deliriously beneath my fingertips as I score, a split second before Keating applies the tag.

"Safe!" the umpire yells, and gives the hands-crossing motion to confirm what he's just said.

"*Safe!*" I yell, and I bounce to my feet in jubilation, choking on the cloud of dirt and not caring at all. "*We did it!*"

Charlie yells, "We won! We won! We won!" He hugs me and then lifts me on his shoulder as the rest of the team spills onto the field.

Everyone is yelling and cheering and slapping me on my back. I'm whooping it up and smiling like I've never smiled before, rejoicing in the cheers not only of my teammates but also the shouts of Mom and Anna from the stands, calling out my name.

And then the great moment gets even greater.

Above all the cheers and yelling, I hear my dad call out, "Way to go, Rabbit!" And then he says the words I've longed for him to say for so long. When things went really bad for us and all we did was argue and shout at each other, I was sure I'd never hear them from him again. Even after his miraculous change and he became *Dad* again, he seemed to have forgotten those magical words.

But now they ring out loud and clear.

"Proud of you, Rabbit!" he shouts. "Proud of you!"

# CHAPTER 18

The whole lot of us—the team, coaches, and fans—decide that pizza at Fauci's is the best way to celebrate. But before we leave the field, Coach Kowalski approaches the stands where I'm talking with my parents and Anna. He isn't wearing the LEHS warm-up suit I'm accustomed to seeing him in. He's wearing a dark suit, white shirt, and tie, much like Dad.

"That was quite a play at the end if the game, Mr. Labelle," Coach Kowalski says to me after I make the introductions. "You are one quick little son of gun."

I think of how he thought of me quite differently not long ago, but remind myself that hatchet got buried as soon as he elevated me to JVs. That is, as soon as Charlie convinced him to elevate me.

"Thank you, sir," I say. "We couldn't get anything going against that knuckleball. With two outs, that seemed like the best chance we were going to get."

Kowalski nods thoughtfully, and absent-mindedly scratches his big paunch. "I was wondering something. Back when you were on first base, and they tried the pitchout. Why weren't you running? Even as fast as you are, they might have had you. Did you sniff it out, or were you just lucky?"

I tell him about how Keating telegraphs how he grips the ball, so I knew that was the one time all day he wasn't throwing a knuckleball. It had to be a fastball and a pitchout.

Kowalski's bushy gray eyebrows shoot up. "Really? You figured that out?"

"Yes, sir," I say. "I try to study those things. It's like Maury Wills says, 'You steal on the pitcher, not the catcher.'"

Kowalski stares at me, astonished. Finally, he says with bemused shake of the head, "So you aren't just a smart aleck with a big mouth."

I'm not quite sure how to respond to that, so I just shrug and smile.

"I guess I was wrong about you," he says.

Even a dope like me knows better than to nod my head and say, "Yes, you were!" even though that's exactly what my brain gleefully thinks.

"Unless you shoot off your mouth next year," he says, "I expect to see you and a couple of your friends on the varsity."

*

After pizza at Fauci's, we drop off Anna and head home. There's only one perfect way to celebrate Dad finally seeing one of my games and watching me score the winning run. I know it's being greedy to ask, but I can't help myself.

"Can we go in the backyard and play catch?" I ask as he pulls the car into the driveway. Dusk is falling, but there's still a bit of light left.

"It's kind of late," he says hesitantly. "The mosquitoes will eat us alive."

I think of all the times back up in Maine, back before everything went bad between us, when we played catch and had a great time doing it. I feel such a longing for that simple, innocent pleasure. For that closeness to him. Especially after his magic words.

*Proud of you!*

I shrug even though he can't see me. "I just thought...you know..."

"Sure!" Dad says. He turns around and smiles. "But I might have to play barehanded. I have no idea where my glove is. It might still be in an unpacked box. I might have even left it up in Maine. But I'd *love* to play catch with you. Even if it's barehanded and the mosquitoes carry me away."

Something deep inside me rejoices. Dad and I have changed so much since the last time we played catch. That had been a time of innocence and, I suppose, ignorance, too, when all I cared about was sports, and I didn't even see the problems in the world around me. Those days are gone. I'm different now.

It's part of growing up, I guess. Leaving the old you behind and trying to emerge a better you. I think I'm a better person now than I was before. At least I hope so.

But this moment right here is one for a brief return to that younger version of myself when all I wanted was for my dad to throw me the ball and make me dive. When he and I just had fun together. Carefree and full of joy. Taking pleasure in the simple act of me stretching out parallel to the ground to make a difficult catch.

Good times.

*Great* times.

I believe with all my heart that Dad and I will keep having great times like this even as life becomes more and more serious the older I get. Maybe we'll drift apart again, but I don't think so. We'll have tough times, but we'll get through them. Somehow. Someway. We'll cling to the special bond that we once had, then lost, and have now reclaimed with an even greater appreciation of how important it is to both of us.

As I get out of the car, I smile at the thought of Dad playing catch barehanded in the falling light. The mosquitoes will descend, I'm sure, but Dad isn't going to have to play barehanded. I've had his glove on the top shelf in my bedroom closet, sitting there all these months.

Waiting for a moment like this.

# Epilogue

It's the Fourth of July weekend, and our family has invited friends over for a backyard barbeque. *My* friends' families. I'm hoping they'll all become *our* friends

I requested this as an early birthday present even though my birthday isn't for another month and a half. Dad didn't quite know what he was getting himself into, thinking it would just be any old barbeque, but he chuckled and shook his head when I specified the friends we'd be inviting over.

So today, under the early July sunny skies, Dad is all smiles as on three different charcoal grills, he cooks cheeseburgers, hot dogs, chicken, and steak for not just our family, but those of Anna, Charlie, and Jessie. The backyard is really too small for all of us, but we're making do in the close confines. Mom has given orders that Dad and I stay away from politics and religion—which only makes sense—so there will be no mention of the capture of Dr. Martin Luther King's assassin, James Earl Ray, or the assassination of Bobby Kennedy, who likely would have been the Democratic candidate for President, and especially no mention of the Vietnam War, all the protests against it, and the upcoming election this fall.

While I was concerned we all might pair off by race—Anna's family and mine conversing on one side of the thick green lawn while Charlie's and Jessie's converse on the other—it isn't that way at all. Instead, we're paired off by gender and age.

The four moms are inside the house, in the kitchen, making potato salad and garden salad and who knows what else. By the sounds of their laughter echoing out here, they're having a merry old time.

Anna's father threatened to be a standoffish stick-in-the-mud for a while—Anna said he initially didn't want to come when he heard that black families would be here—but even he has come around. Now, the four dads are clustered around the three charcoal grills, sitting on green lawn chairs, slathering barbeque sauce on the meat, drinking beer, and arguing over whether Bill Russell is the greatest Boston athlete of all time or Ted Williams, with Jessie's dad saying that this young defenseman on the Bruins, Bobby Orr, could someday outdo all of them, a comment that earns him hoots of derisive, though playful, laughter.

That leaves us young'uns, as Charlie's mom calls us: Anna and her older brother, Charlie and his younger brother and sister, Jessie, and me. As the smell of the cooking meats fills the air and makes us salivate, we eat chips and dip out of bowls on one of two picnic tables Dad set up just for today. We drink Coca-Cola, toss around a football and a Frisbee, and talk about anything and everything. Except politics and religion.

"You know I was gonna get a hit when you raced home with the winning run," Charlie says to me with a playful grin. "You just a hot dog that had to be the hero."

"Get a hit?" I say with the air of off-the-charts incredulity. "You'd struck out three times. I saved you from embarrassing yourself a fourth!"

"And what did you do to get on base, hot shot?" he asks. "You struck out! Some kind of hero!"

We laugh long and hard.

The barbeque smells and the sounds of laughter and conversation fill the air. But even better, far better for me, is the warm glow of brotherhood between us all.

*

A few weeks later, Anna and I walk hand-in-hand to our seats in the partially darkened, mostly empty movie theater. It's a Saturday matinee and we're here so early the previews haven't even started. We're here to see *The Odd Couple*, a comedy starring Jack Lemmon and Walter Matthau. Lemmon plays a neat freak who moves in with Matthau, a slob, and together, they drive each other crazy. It's supposed to be really funny, but to be honest, it could just as well be the Bugs Bunny Saturday morning cartoons. What matters is that I'm here with Anna.

On our first date.

Mom just dropped us off, then will pick us up after the movie and take us to a nice restaurant called the Tides down the Causeway from Lynn into Nahant. The Tides overlooks the Atlantic Ocean, and is supposed to have great Italian food and seafood, but who cares about that?

It'll just be Anna and me. On our first date. McDonald's or roast beef sandwiches at Bill and Bob's would still be great.

The agreement that Mom—the Best Mom Ever!—worked out with Anna's parents—mostly Anna's mom, I think—is that we don't leave the theatre or restaurant without her. That way it's carefully supervised because, as we've been told a hundred billion times, we're only fourteen.

But we're still alone. On our first date!

I can't believe it! When Mom said she'd set it up, then asked with a sly look on her face if I was interested, I practically jumped out of my skin. Interested? Of course I was interested!

And now here we are in our seats. Holding hands. Leaning against each other.

My heart feels like it's about to pound itself out of my chest. Since the previews haven't started yet, music is playing, but nothing is up on the screen. I'm so nervous I can't think of anything to say.

"Your hair smells nice," I blurt out, and then want to slap myself for saying something so stupid.

I'm such a moron. Could I possibly have come up with anything that sounded any more ridiculous? I doubt it. Even though the strawberry scent of her hair is really nice, and so is the lilac smell of her perfume.

"Thank you," Anna says, then looks at me with a sly grin. Behind her maroon-framed glasses, her brown eyes twinkle. "And your odor is…quite tolerable."

We burst out laughing.

God, how I love this girl!

We both eat some of the buttered popcorn out of the bucket we're sharing and wash it down with a sip of our extra-large Coke. The popcorn is a little too salty, but who cares? Every last kernel could be burnt to a crisp and it wouldn't matter.

I'm with the best girl ever.

On our first date.

"Rabbit," Anna says, whispering softly so only the two of us can hear her even though no one is sitting anywhere close to us yet. She leans close so her shoulder-length blond hair brushes my cheek. I know from her tone that what's coming next is no joke. She's serious. I swallow hard, hoping it's something good.

"I know you've been a hero lots of times on your sports teams," she says. "Like scoring the winning run in the championship baseball game, and all your touchdowns on the football team."

My mouth feels dry as cotton, but now isn't the time for slurping Coke. This doesn't sound good. I wait on pins and needles.

"I just want you to know that I don't love you because you're a sports hero," Anna says. "I don't even love you because you were a hero for choosing right over wrong during the basketball protests or all the other times."

She gives my hand a squeeze, and the lump in my throat feels like it's the size of a watermelon.

"I love you," she says, "because you're you."

I look into those beautiful brown eyes, and lower my head to hers.

Our lips touch and for the first time…

…I kiss the softest, sweetest lips in the universe.

Once. Twice. A third time.

They taste of spearmint and butter.

Something tells me, we might not see a lot of this movie.

**The Rabbit Labelle Saga**

*Offside*
*Offensive Foul*
*Bottom of the Ninth*


And if you enjoyed the Rabbit Labelle books,
please consider *Cracking the Ice*,
which tells what happens next to Jessie Stackhouse.

# Acknowledgements

Thanks to the many friends who helped me get details right, most recently Jen Mahoney and Charlie Mahoney. Over the course of all the Rabbit Labelle books, it's been close to the entire Lynn English Class of 1974. I may need a bank loan for my bar tab at the next reunion.

To my awesome first readers, who once again provided me with great insights, as they have done for every book in the series.

To my editor, Dayle Dermatis, whose expertise caught countless mistakes. Any typos or errors that remain are entirely my own fault.

To my son, Ryan, for the initial inspiration for Rabbit, that sports-crazed kid who just couldn't get enough.

To all my friends and family, for their love and support.

But most of all, to the Best Wife Ever and the love of my life, Brenda. For everything!

# About the Author

David H. Hendrickson's first novel, *Cracking the Ice*, was praised by *Booklist* as "a gripping account of a courageous young man rising above evil." He has since published six additional novels, including *Offside* (the first book in the Rabbit Labelle series), which has been adopted for high school student required reading.

His short fiction has appeared in *Best American Mystery Stories 2018*, *Ellery Queen's Mystery Magazine*, *Heart's Kiss*, multiple issues of *Pulphouse Fiction Magazine*, and numerous anthologies, including more than a half dozen issues of *Fiction River*. He is a multi-finalist for the Derringer Award, and his story "Death in the Serengeti" was honored with the 2018 Derringer Award for Best Long Story.

Pentucket Publishing has released two of his short story collections, *Shimmers and Laughs: Eight Wildly Hilarious Tales* and *Death in the Serengeti and Other Stories: Ten Tales of Crime.*

Hendrickson has published over fifteen hundred works of nonfiction, most notably his first book for writers, *How to Get Your Book into Schools and Double Your Income with Volume Sales*, and also *Travis Roy: Quadriplegia and a Life of Purpose*. He has been honored with the Joe Concannon Hockey East Media Award and the Murray Kramer Scarlet Quill Award.

Visit him online at www.hendricksonwriter.com.

## A Special Request From the Author

Word of mouth is crucial for any author to succeed. If you enjoyed this book, please consider leaving a review where you purchased it. Even if it's only a line or two, it would make all the difference and would be very much appreciated.